ABYSS

STORIES OF DEPTH, TIME AND INFINITY

EDITED BY

C.R. DUDLEY

ORCHID'S
LANTERN

Published by Orchid's Lantern Limited
North Yorkshire, UK
www.orchidslantern.com

ISBN (paperback): 978-1-999-8684-6-8
ISBN (ebook): 978-1-999-8684-7-5

Cover design, editing and typesetting by Orchid's Lantern

"And if thou gaze long into an abyss, the abyss will also gaze into thee."

Friedrich Nietzsche

Contents

The Memory Hole

R. A. Busby

Memory is a funny thing, isn't it?

Do you remember that 1983 Rob Lowe film *I Regret Nothing*? Rob plays a down-on-his-luck office drone who finds a winning lottery ticket on the subway and invites his dream girl Helen Slater to Paris, hoping to impress her. It wasn't a major blockbuster, but it had a great soundtrack with this killer song by the Thompson Twins I haven't been able to find anywhere else.

You might not recall the movie, but I sure do. I saw it in the theater when I was fifteen, and during the climactic make-up scene in the Louvre, my date Traci Jorgenson took my hand and let me feel an actual girl's breast for the first time in my life, so I've been a big Rob Lowe fan ever since.

Yeah, I regret nothing.

The thing is, you probably *don't* remember the movie.

Only twelve people ever claimed otherwise, but it mostly turned out they'd confused it with some other early 80s flick, maybe *Oxford Blues* or *Class*. Still, one guy on Reddit uploaded a picture of the VHS tape he'd found in his parents' basement, and there it was, same as I have, with the pink cover, the Eiffel Tower, and all.

But that's it. Search all you want to on IMDb and you won't find this film. Go ahead. Try it. But if you do, would you let me know? My name is Nick Day, and my address is in the back of this journal you're holding in your hands.

Please contact me. Really, as soon as possible.

I've got the movie locked in my bedroom safe between my journal and my favorite work by the Doors, a live small-venue concert album called *Highway 49* that Jim Morrison recorded less than two years before he died. On the album, he duets with Eric Burdon on 'House of the Rising Sun,' followed by 'Cocaine Blues,' and this old sea shanty, 'Fair Spanish Ladies.' All I can say is that those dudes took the roof off the house. Amazing.

You don't remember this either?

All right, so here's one you possibly do recall. What are the last words for Queen's 'We Are the Champions'?

Ah. Now we're talking.

The funny thing is, though, not everybody remembers it that way.

I'm just an ordinary middle-aged book editor, definitely not a science guy, but for some time I've been researching what people call the Mandela Effect. It's a phenomenon named after the anti-Apartheid leader who died in 1988 of tuberculosis in Pollsmore Prison, and who also served as president of South Africa from 1994 to 1999.

Most only remember the second event. A few remember both. I'm one of them.

The day Mandela died got carved into my brain because my freshman roommate Richard's family had been forcibly relocated to Soweto in the 50s, and Richard must have played the song 'Free Nelson Mandela' about a hundred times after we heard the news. We talked about it until four in the morning. Naturally, I was quite shocked when Mandela won the South African presidency six years later.

I told myself I'd simply misremembered. Our memories are flexible, you see. Five minutes' research into the reliability of crime eyewitnesses will show you that. We can implant details into other people's consciousness, create false recollections—hell, even trick ourselves. Sometimes, we are our own best gaslighters.

But then came the Stephen King thing. No, I'm not his number-one fan (heh-heh-heh), but I've been on Team Constant Reader since age ten when I ripped off *Carrie* from the school library because my mom wouldn't let me see the movie. I recall being bummed as hell in 1999 after that fatal van accident, thinking I'd never read a new King book again once his publisher ran out of old trunk novels.

Surprise.

Until the Internet really took off, I thought I was alone. As it happened, other folks recalled these events as well, which is where the term 'Mandela Effect' came from: it's when many people remember a specific thing occurring when it really didn't.

Except it did.

Oh, people get facts wrong. We misremember, conflate, or simply fail to pay attention. Happens all the time. Bogie never uttered the line, 'Play it again, Sam.' Vader never said, 'Luke, I am your father,' and the Fruit of the Loom logo never featured a cornucopia.

But I remember what I remember.

I have to.

You see, memory is all we really are.

Around when I saw Stephen King's live interviews for *Dreamcatcher*, proving definitively that he was Not Dead, I began a diary. A modest work at first, merely a method to keep track. For reasons I think you'll understand, I don't trust computers. Sure, I use them, but their essential fluidity of information is troubling. Especially on the Internet, knowledge can simply disappear forever down the memory hole. No, I prefer yellowing newspapers, chunky plastic VHS tapes, the hairline grooves of a record album housed in a worn cardboard sleeve. These things exist. They are tangible. They last, or I hope they do.

But maybe not. Anyway, the best theory I've heard explaining the cause of the Mandela Effect goes as follows.

You've probably read about the Large Hadron Collider, an enormous circular tunnel 27 kilometers long. Scientists accelerate protons through this space until they whiz along at close to light speed—the protons, not the scientists. Think of an autobahn for subatomic particles. Anyway, the protons are on a crash course with other protons, and when they smack into each other, the collision creates conditions resembling those found in the early universe. Despite some initial concerns—*It'll melt like Chernobyl! It'll cause a black hole!*—the experiments proceeded safely.

Well, until some weird shit happened.

In 2011, after the LHC had been online a few years, scientists recorded a particle collision taking place *before* the event occurred. Effect before cause. Why did this happen? From what I've been able to determine, the general scientific consensus seems to be, 'We don't really know.' One possibility is the collider initiated a fundamental shift in reality. Each experiment may have caused our universe to clone itself, as if some drunk hit 'copy/paste' 38498549345 times by accident on a booty call. And, from the moment the universes split, they diverged. In one clone-iverse, perhaps, the particle collision occurred ever-so-slightly earlier than in ours.

But the problem was this: How come the collision event jumped ship from Universe A to Universe B? Had these experiments created a connecting tunnel between realities? Possibly many tunnels? And if so— well. What were the implications of that?

And, um … which were we in?

We don't really know.

I realize how this sounds.

Even online I try not to talk about it, not directly. The Internet may be a rich storehouse of information, but it's also a giant manure pile in which crazy conspiracy theories flourish like intellectual kudzu. For the record, I believe we *did* land on the moon, Oswald *did* shoot JFK, birds are real, and Earth is spherical. I do *not* think 9/11 was an inside job, or Democrats drink baby blood, or Ted Cruz is the Zodiac Killer.

For fuck's sake, people.

When Mandela won the election in '94, though, these ideas were all new to me. I tried contacting my old roommate Richard to see if he remembered what I did, even wheedling his contact information out of the university alumni secretary, but Richard never responded. About a year later, his parents sent me a brief letter explaining he was dead.

Okay, so from what I can tell, there are at least four basic groups. Some folks remember Mandela's death. A smaller number recall Stephen King's, including a man from Bangor who photographed himself by the pile of flowers left at King's mansion with those distinctive spiderweb gates. Only the Reddit guy and I have seen *I Regret Nothing*, but then again, the movie wasn't that memorable. Then there's the rest—the vast majority who remember the past the way you're supposed to. I'm the only person in every group.

Over time, I've come to think I just got left over, human lint trapped in the dryer after the old tenants moved out. Along with the Doors album and the Rob Lowe movie, your man Nick Day is just a forgotten physical remnant of these four diverging timelines. I'm a memento.

I'll tell you, it gets confusing sometimes. This journal

helps, especially since I've learned the hard way to keep my ideas to myself. My marriage foundered in 2005 after I risked telling my wife Sandra about my—well, let's call them my diverging temporal experiences. Sandra has always been an extremely rational person, a major reason I fell in love with her, and in the many discussions that followed, she advanced all the calm, intelligent objections you'd expect.

Even when I showed her the evidence from my safe— the VHS tape, the Morrison album—her explanations were clear and reasonable. IMDb cataloguing omissions. Rediscovered works. Bootlegs. Elaborate fakes constructed to part the unwary from their paychecks. Despite our arguments over the next year, I respected the hell out of her. Sandra only wanted me to believe what she thought was the truth.

But memory is all we really have. Memory is all we really are. And in the end, it cost me more than a paycheck. Sandra stuck to her guns; I stuck to mine, and pretty soon, we were facing each other over a long conference table with his-and-hers attorneys, hashing out a custody arrangement for Nicky Junior, our five-year-old son.

Looming over it all was the threat of my being deemed cognitively unfit, especially since I have a troublesome family history with my dad and grandpa in that regard. I may have told you this already, but something happened to them later in life. Sandra didn't know—hell, I barely knew all the facts myself—but even a bus-bench attorney could do a little digging, if they were so inclined. Why give them a reason?

With these considerations in mind, I agreed to Sandra's stipulations, which (naturally) were reasonable. Bottom line, I'd already lost my wife. I didn't want to lose my son. Sandra was my love, but Nicky is my heart.

All the same, I remember what I remember.

At least I kept my job. For more than a decade, I've worked as a textbook editor for—well, you'd recognize the company. Hell, you doubtlessly used our materials. You might even have killed time in some boring American history class by scrawling dicks on the page with *Washington Crossing the Delaware* in our very book. I literally had a kid from Olathe, Kansas send my office a laminated version of one he'd drawn, labeled and everything. God, people are strange.

And no, the irony of my work does not escape me. My job is to check that the facts in the American history product line remain consistent—that is, to ensure Washington's Delaware crossing occurs on Christmas in 1776, for example. You'd think this process would be easy, but it's not. After all, history gets rewritten all the time. Reworded introductions, new material, and changing social outlooks all affect the content your kids read in school. For every gain, there's usually some loss.

For the past year, though, it's gotten harder to keep the timelines straight, even with this journal. The discrepancies between the parallel realities have been increasing recently. A lot. This worries me. I imagine not a singular wormhole connecting the universes, but some ugly, sprawling, spaghetti-bowl tangle, protons passing everywhere and everywhen, fucking things up beyond repair.

Worse, my work is suffering. I am becoming less sure of what I am officially supposed to believe. It used to be easier. Nelson Mandela was not dead; he was South Africa's leader from 1994 to 1999. Stephen was still King, long may he reign. No Lowe flick, no Morrison album. Gotcha.

But things are changing.

Did I already tell you that?

Yesterday, my supervisor Gary called me into the office. After a few preliminaries—was I doing all right? How was Nicky?—he got down to the Elphabas Farber issue.

'I was looking over your edits,' said Gary, 'and usually, they're spot-on. Spot-on. You're a pro, Nick. No doubt this is a minor thing. Anyway, I noticed you made some corrections here.'

He shifted his second monitor so I could read over his shoulder. Gary had opened the file for the chapter called 'Forging a New Democracy,' which detailed the history behind the Declaration of Independence. Some junior copywriter had written that there were 57 signers, and although this was a rookie mistake, I was glad I'd caught it. You have no idea how many pissy emails we get from teachers for every little thing. No idea.

'Yeah.' I frowned.

'So where's Elphabas Farber?' Gary spread his arms wide, as if he expected some tricorned Revolutionary War figure to leap into them like a grateful bride.

'Sorry?'

'Very amusing, Nick,' Gary laughed. 'I realize he's no Button Gwinnett, but we can't just leave him out. Anyway, I wanted to tell you why I was sending these chapters back, but here's a heads-up, buddy—we've got to sign off on this part, so I'm looking forward to the fixes by about two o'clock. Too early?'

Forcing my face to smile, I agreed the corrections would be in Gary's inbox by noon. In the meantime, I had to figure out a crucial question: Who the hell was Elphabas Farber? Thank God for Wikipedia.

The fact was, I couldn't tell Gary there have always been 56 signers. 56. No more. No fewer. And Elphabas Farber wasn't among them.

In my universe, at least.

If I can just keep everything straight, it'll be okay. This journal will be a giant history manuscript in progress, complete with red lines, additions, omissions, cross-outs and above all, 'Track Changes.' I have to track the changes. I have to track the changes in the timelines, perhaps with color-coding. Note to self: Buy highlighters at the store.

~

Things Known:

1. Right now, there are 50 states, 5 major ~~terrortories~~ territories.

2. There are 118 elements in the periodic table. I have begun to memorize them in case something shifts. I can confidently recall each

element up to arsenic (#33).

3. In all timelines experienced so far, my name is Nick Day, I work at a textbook company, my ex-wife is Sandra, and my little boy is Nick, Jr.

4. In all timelines, Nick's favorite song is 'I Can See Clearly Now,' by Bobby McFerrin. Before starting kindergarten at Samuel Chase ES, Nick was afraid the kids wouldn't be friends with him. To make Nick feel happy, I put on this song before I took him to school for the first time and together, we danced away the blues. I'll always recall him, my perfect son bouncing around the room to the beat, blue backpack sliding off his shoulders, and the high, pure sound of his laughter. I lifted him into my arms and waltzed with my son awhile as we sang. After I let Nicky out at school and saw him swallowed up by the building, I cried a little in my car and drove home by myself

5. There are 56 57 signers of the Declaration. I think.

~

Journal with me always. Getting hard to recognize what changes to track. I recorded all the titles of books I have on my shelves, but my hand hurts like a bitch. I ended up taking photos, but who knows what will happen to them? Later, when I went out on a run in the afternoon to clear my head up a bit, I noticed my neighbor repainted the trim on her house.

Or has it always been that way?

I came home right now, and my TV is different.

~

Things Known:

145. Tellurium, iodine, xenon, cesium, barium, lanthanum, cerium, praseodymium

146. Thirty days hath September
April, June, and November
All the rest have thirty-one
Save for February alone,
Which hath four and twenty-four
Till leap year gives it one day more.

147. Please Excuse My Dear Aunt Sally

148. ~~My Very Good Boy~~ Every Good Boy Does Fine

149. Is Pluto a planet? Must verify.

~

It was Friday afternoon, so I was waiting in the parking lot outside Samuel Chase ES, Nicky's elementary school, watching the little kids spill out of the building and climb into buses. From where I sat, I could see the front gates decently enough, so I kept my eye out for my son's head, dark as a seal bobbing above the water. As the flood of kids thinned out, I didn't spot him. No kids with a blue backpack in the right shade. Finally, the last buses pulled away, and although a few students waited on the benches for their moms and dads, none was Nick.

After twenty minutes, I walked to the main office, hoping they could page him or something. He was doubtlessly hanging out with his friends or talking to some teacher, but if we were going to catch the movie I'd planned to surprise him with, we'd have to make tracks.

As I came in, the secretary looked up from her computer.

'Hi,' I said, glancing awkwardly at the color-coded files, the stiff and self-important row of binders behind her. 'Can you please page a student? You know, over the intercom or something?'

'Absolutely.' She smiled and reached for the handset. 'What's the child's name?'

I told her, and she frowned. The phone slowly lowered. 'I don't recall a Nick Day.'

'Nicholas, then. Or Nicky?'

The frown did not disappear. Turning away, she ran her fingers over the keyboard.

'Very sorry, sir,' she answered, and now all the cheer had left her voice. 'We do not have a student by that name.'

Sandra must have withdrawn him. Taken him to another school? A private school? A charter?

But why not tell me?

Oh, Jesus, please let Nicky be okay. Please let Nicky be okay. Please let Nicky be okay.

The second I got back to the car, I called Sandra. Nicky

was fine, she said. Did I want to talk to him? She'd just gotten off the phone two minutes ago, and he sounded great.

Now it was my turn to frown.

'Why would you be—is Nick spending the night at a friend's? I mean, you could've told me, San. I waited for an hour in the Chase parking lot before going to the office, and the secretary—she may be new or something, but anyway, she didn't page him because his name wasn't on file, so you can imagine, I—'

But then she asked why I would be waiting for Nicky at all.

I explained it was Friday, and she agreed this was the case (thankfully). There was an uncomfortable pause.

Why, she inquired, had I been waiting at his old elementary school when Nick was a freshman in college?

~

Things Known:

456. My Very Excellent Mother Just Served Us Nine ~~Pizzas~~

457. PEMDAS

459. Thorium, protactinium, plutonium, uranium, neptunium, americium

459. Nicky is a college freshman

460. Willie, Willie, Harry, Stee, Harry, Dick, John, Harry III

458. 57 signers of the Delaware

455.   Nicky is a college freshman

~

Yesterday, my supervisor called me into the office. Following a few banal exchanges—how was I doing? How was Nick?—he got down to the problem of a Mr Elphabas Farber.

'I was taking a little look-see at your edits,' said Gary. 'You're a pro, Nick. Everybody makes mistakes. I'm sure this is a minor thing.'

He shifted his third monitor so I could read over his shoulder. Some junior copywriter had put down that there were 56 signers, and they'd left off one guy.

'Yeah.' I frowned, staring up at Gary.

'So who's Elphabas Farber?'

'Sorry?'

'Very funny, Nick,' Gary chuckled. 'I think some intern was trying to see if you really read these docs before you pass them on. God, can you imagine the pissy emails we'd get from teachers if we hadn't caught that? Hell, half of them think we made up the name Button Gwinnett. Anyway, wanted to let you understand why I was shooting these chapters back to you, but here's a heads-up—we've got to sign off on this part, so I'll look forward to getting the fixes by about eleven o'clock. Too early?'

I told him eleven would be fine.

At my desk, I checked Wikipedia.

~~57~~ 56 signers.

~

Things Known:

    1005. 118 elements ending with oganesson. The word looks like a blank-faced man with a slit for a mouth. Can't remember the elements after 55. Must review list.

           55 is the atomic number for cesium. 55 is the age Caesar died. Cesium. Barium. I have come to barium cesium, not to praseodymium.

    1006. The wormholes are spaghetti.
           83409584993485 universes. I think they're getting tangled. Some are collapsing into each other. Copy/paste.

    1002. Track changes.

~

Time's been on my mind lately.

I finally figured out how the new TV works, so I checked the news. It's December 20, 2019. Almost Delaware-crossing time. Anyway, I have a theory I haven't shared on Reddit or TikTok.

(Note: Has TikTok been invented yet? Must check.)

It goes this way. Einstein theorized time moves like a river, at least from our perspective. Throwing something into the stream would only affect things downstream from you, so simply put, the present affects only the future, not the past. One direction.

But what if time is actually a pond?

If I stand by a pond and toss in a rock, the ripples don't move in one direction. They move outward in all directions. Eventually, the waves come right back to me and lap my feet.

What if events in the future were screwing things up in the past? Effect before cause. But with the way universes seem to be snarling like bad yarn, I can't help worrying whether some enormous rock landed in the pond up ahead, a huge boulder making a big-ass splash in the timeline, sending not just ripples back into the past, but waves.

If I don't keep track of everything, what if it vanishes forever? We've already lost Pluto, for Chrissakes. I realize it was the smallest, but it still fucking *matters*, guys.

What's going to happen now?

~

I can't find my car.

~

'For the fourteenth time,' I told the cop, although I didn't remember if it really was the fourteenth, 'I was there to pick up my son from school. His name is Nicholas Day, Jr. No, I don't understand why the secretary called you. No, I don't recall the office assistant telling me to leave several times before—hell, I don't recollect it at all. Maybe you should haul *her* in here for filing a false report or disturbing the peace, or whatever.'

The officer's hair was shiny-dark and reminded me of Nicky's, but his expression was stern, or at least as stern as a young man's could get. Christ, he looked barely old enough to shave, which is probably why he was on elementary-school duty. Just graduated from hall monitor, I guess.

'Mr—ah,' said the cop. We were sitting in the principal's conference room at Nicky's school staring at a wall full of framed motivational posters. One showed a brightly colored sprout emerging from the soil, and below it read the slogan, 'The Future Depends on What You Do Today.' *Not necessarily*, I thought.

'Day,' I said to the cop. 'Nick Day.' Sergeant Hall Monitor peered at the license I'd given him, and I told him my address and where I worked. 'Am I under arrest?' I asked at last, impatient with the silence and the posters.

'No,' the cop admitted, 'but sir, I'm concerned since—'

'Am I being detained?'

Sgt Monitor gave an apologetic shrug. 'Certainly not, but you should know we've called someone who—'

'Am I free to go?'

'Well, yes, but Mr Day, because you can't seem to locate your vehicle, the admin has provided us with a contact number for you based on the last time you came here, and I strongly suggest you simply wait in this office unt—'

'So I am free to go?'

'Yes, but—'

'Fuck you, then.' I rose and pushed away my chair, but standing at the door of the conference room was a man of about my height and build. I stared at him, mouth agape, before turning back to Sgt Monitor, who was gathering up his pens and pad. 'Excuse me,' I demanded, jabbing a finger at the new arrival. 'What kind of bullshit is this?'

Sgt Monitor glanced to the man and back to me, blue eyes wide and guileless. 'Very sorry, Mr Day, but I can't see what you—'

'Him.' I pointed again. 'I am talking about *him*. And don't lie to me—I'm not fooled by whatever bullshit you're trying to pull here, Sergeant. I know you see him too. You or the agency you're working with—was it CERN? You fixed it. You fixed the divergent timelines.'

'What—sir, would you please—'

'Your agents at CERN—you spliced the timelines back together, but you fucked up, Sergeant. You dumbasses left me out of the splice, didn't you? You didn't *splice* me; you *cloned* me, and now—'

'I really don't understand what—' The sergeant flicked his glance to the man at the door, who came closer.

'What I want to know is this.' I leaned in close enough to smell the sergeant's aftershave. 'I'm the missing detail that couldn't be spliced back, aren't I? What are you here for? To erase your mistake, *Men in Black*-style? How did you people do it? *How did you finally splice the timelines, you asshole*?'

By now, the intruder grasped me gently by the shoulders and turned me around. I knew the face well enough.

Hell, I should. I see it in the mirror every morning.

Then he spoke. 'Dad,' he said in my voice. 'Dad, we're here.'

The doctor sat in a comfortable chair, her sensible heels

reminding me of Sandra. She had a little tattoo on her ankle that resembled a knotted string, and she wore the surgical blue mask that seems to be the fashion nowadays.

She asked me the date. I told her it was December. She made a note in her journal, and I wondered if she color-coded her entries as well. 'Where do you think we are, Mr Day?' she inquired, and I said we were in her office.

The doctor then said, 'Do you know who the President is?' and on that, my mind blanked. The first president was Washington crossing the Delaware. The fourteenth president was Lincoln. The 45th element is rhodium. Then the answer came to me. 'The email lady,' I responded. At the doctor's look of surprise, visible even above her mask, I quickly realized I was in error. 'Fine.' I threw up my hands. 'Then who is it?' She gave me an answer.

'Stop fucking with me,' I told her.

They say it's my room. It is not. It's *a* room, but it is not mine. My doppelganger comes to visit me every week, his dark hair falling across his forehead the way my own does. I can't recall how long I've been here. Time seems to have puddled in this last year, slowing down, becoming a sticky Higgs field in which we're all wading as through quicksand. Days flow into days (no pun intended), so as they say on Reddit, ask me anything. Is it Tuesday? December? Could be. 1983? Why not?

I ask my Nick Day doppelganger about the tape and the album, the ones in my safe, but he shakes his head gently and says that he's very sorry, but he doesn't know what I mean. He smooths my hair back from my forehead and kisses me there.

If my safe still exists, if Sandra figured out the combination (my birthday), then she either kept the contents around for old times' sake, or she sold them at a garage sale. Hell, that's where I found the album and the tape in the first place, so if she did, at least it would have a fitting circularity to it. A kind of roundness.

They merged the timelines. Stopped the ripple in the pond. They'd done so much. So much, but they didn't get it all, not everything. Not all the swimmers make it to the lifeboat, if you know what I mean. Erase all you want to, but some of the pencil marks stay behind. Like a memento. I am a memento.

And I remember.

I remember the taste of popcorn on Traci Jorgenson's lips, the light salty overlay on top of her candy-flavored gloss. I remember the feel of her breast nestling in my hand like a warm little bird. I remember Morrison and Mandela and dancing with my beautiful boy, blue backpack bouncing, and the weight of him in my arms as we waltzed to Bobby McFerrin. I remember everything, because memory is all we really have. It's all we really are.

I'm still here, even though I don't exist. And if you're reading this … well.

You may not exist either.

That's okay.

I regret nothing.

Static

Merl Fluin

The face is white, bone white, but the hair is black. Grey at the roots. Vain old fart.

Whole caravan's been picked clean already. My own fault, you snooze you lose. Shame. I reckon he had some nice titbits stashed away.

Whoever swagged it all left him untouched in his bed, though. Too chickenshit to check a dead body for jewellery. Superstitious pricks. It's stupid to be scared of a dead body.

Of course it is.

Freezing in here, moonlight's like a fridge. See my own breath. The tatty eiderdown smells odd, sugary. It's pulled up to his chin.

Fuck me, he's wearing make-up. Long flicks of eye-liner, streaks of gold on the lids, Tutankhamun-style. Well, each to their own, I'm not prejudiced. But lying here as if he knew he was about to die, as if he was settling down to wait for it? As if he'd dolled himself up especially to meet it?

Ok, get it over with. Hold my breath, pull back the covers.

Christ, he's beautiful. Veined, streaked, like Renaissance marble. You think a corpse will be matt grey, but he's teeming with colours, green, blue, crimson. He has a sheen to him.

There's something on his breastbone, about the length of my palm, shiny, slender. Phone torch, let's have a proper look.

Jackpot.

It's a rabbit's foot, a lucky charm. White fur, the claws are pearly. At the other end—rabbit's ankle, I guess—it's set in a metal tube studded with three chunky stones. No hallmark on the silver, but now I look closer there's a lot of engraving, swirly lines, could be some kind of script, Arabic or something Indian. Looks handmade, crafted. Might be worth money. Yes, old fella, thank you very much, I'll have a bit of this.

Try not to touch—urgh. His skin's squishy, meaty.

Fuck this, get out of here, get out quick.

Broken door, cold moon, steps, stumble, sick as a pup. My skull's full of water, too heavy to lift. Belly sloshes. Swallow, boy, don't chuck up. Chest feels like my heart's sprouted teeth. Keep it together, that's it, give it a few minutes, just breathe. Powder-white on the exhale. Couple of dogs barking over the way. A few windows glitter in the distance, but in this field everything's still. Moon up there pale and full as the earth down here, frozen twins, doppelgängers. All right now, let's go home. Squeaking on the snow as I double back to my pitch, white claws sharp against my palm. Static caravans in rows like hutches.

She sits down at the end of the bed, the mattress dips as my hard-on rises, here she is, my lovely, my warm, my Suzanne.

No, that's not right.

She's not here. I'm not there. Because. Because I did. That thing. Remember, don't remember. No more home. I live like this now.

Wake up.

Everything dapples yellow–orange, like a faded childhood Kodak snap. Back of my mouth fizzes. Phone says 03:33. Specks of shadow buzz and flit, a tangerine light show. I'm having a fit, only I can't be, haven't had one of those since I was a kid. Screw my eyes shut, wait for the fizzing to stop. Thin foam pitches under my legs again, and if Walker's fucking cat has got in here and shat everywhere I swear to Christ I'll kill it for real this time, but look, it's not a cat. It's a boy.

Five or six years old, dark eyes, dark curls. Red corduroy trousers and an orange skinny-rib jumper that looks hand-knit, familiar. Fizz in my mouth turns to acid tang. 'How did you get in here?'

Pulls his feet up beneath him and gazes at me, cross-legged. 'I've come from the future.'

This dream is particularly stupid.

'Oh yeah? What's the future like, smart-arse?'

'Don't you remember?'

I'm not fucking having this. 'I don't know what you're meant to be, but you can fuck off. Right now.'

He doesn't flinch. Fair play to him, the little shit. I can smell him now, too: garish sweets, soda pop.

'I know you,' he says. 'You stole treasure.'

Shit. This isn't a dream. Must be someone's little brother. They were watching the old fella's caravan and they saw me come out with something they'd missed, so they've sent this nipper to get it.

Or it's me they've been watching, following me about, spying, stalking me.

Shit.

The light swoops and dances, colour of sunshine through closed fingers. There's a roaring in my head.

'I mean it. Get to fuck or I'll give you the hiding you're asking for.'

Grab the belt from the pile of last night's clothes on the floor. Come on, kid, this has to be a nightmare, why don't you vanish now like you're supposed to? His eyes dart around the room, to the door, to the window. I'm after him with belt held high, déjà vu, father and son. He's on his feet, balance uncertain on the mattress, twists to grasp the wardrobe handles behind him. I can easily reach him from here, with or without the belt. Little bunny, I could eat you alive. But he's already got the wardrobe open, kicks himself off into the dark space. A flash of his blue nylon football socks and the wardrobe door clicks shut.

Well, then. He's going nowhere. Only route out of there is back through that wardrobe door. Let him sweat. Or let big bruv come and fetch him. I'm ready either way. Sick of everyone's bullshit.

Make myself a Nescafé and take it back to bed. The rabbit's foot, the boy's treasure, is still on the bedside unit where I left it. Switch on the lamp, inspect it again. Turn it round and round, the gemstones glow, sumptuous and deep, blue, yellow and red. Definitely seen that script somewhere before. Art school, funny little teacher, what was her name, always laughing. Sanskrit? Big coffee table book of Buddhist art Suzanne gave me one birthday, some of it had writing looked like that. Gorgeous book, that was. My life was gorgeous then. These tarsal bones, so delicate, so frail behind the soft white fur. When you look underneath there's almost no paw there at all. I remember the pet rabbit I had as a child, the leathery pads of its little feet, but this is just gristle. How I sobbed when that rabbit died. I bawled for weeks. Kids are such morons. Ollie must be asleep right now. This coffee's foul.

Enough. Time for lights out.

The world outside the window blazes fierce and clear. I can see across the whole caravan park. The snowflakes hang above it but never seem to reach the ground. The man in the moon, I've heard in some countries they say it's a hare. My eyesight blurs and the falling snow goes gently haywire, begins to rise instead of fall, rising and rising. The earth swivels on its axis, black water cascades through my head, everything ripples in the wrong direction. A curtain rising to reveal a secret that's been hidden in plain sight. I hear the wardrobe open, but I can't tear my eyes from the snow. My perception's adrift like the fuzz between stations on a transistor radio. The little red plastic transistor I used to hide under my bedclothes deep into the night. You let it slip out of focus and something else starts to crystallize, something other.

I feel the boy slide warm beneath the duvet and touch my forearm, a frail prickly touch. He snuggles against my bare chest. His head is downy. That sweet hay smell. My throat spasms and I know I'm watched. I hold back the tears. The jumper is every bit as scratchy as I remember. Mum could only afford cheap acrylic yarn. It was my favourite all the same, because I loved the colour. I don't understand. I try to clutch the rabbit's foot but I can't find my hands.

Again a twitch of the mattress. Someone or something at the end of the bed. Doughy palms distort against the frame, fingers grip the sheet, the dead old man slides himself out from underneath me.

Up he glides, out and up, impossibly tall, like a rising snow bank, until he looms over me where I lie with the three jewels cold in my hand and my childhood self nestled beneath my heart. His corpse flames with colours, red, blue, yellow, the gold gleam of his eyes, his hair wild and black as mine.

With wet fingers he points at his own breastbone. The hair on the boy's head burrows into my flesh, warm and squirmy. My ribcage unfurls to embrace him. I'm being pulled wide open so the light from the dead man's body floods it all. My body is a gaping pocket of white fur.

Above the bright full earth I rise. Child, man, corpse, I watch over them from up here and I know I can never love them enough, my past lives, my future deaths, all the lives and deaths of the world, the love gouges and scrapes me hollow. Make it stop. Agony, this love is agony. Stop it, please stop it, I'm begging. Stop it, let me go, drop me back to the ground.

Plastic wristband, hospital smell, dirty hair. Hushed voices in the waiting room, things that can't be said out loud, the way grown-ups talk behind a child's back. How much fucking longer? The porter trundled me in here at lunchtime, and now it's starting to get dark. I could walk out and take the bus home. No, on second thoughts better stay and wait for patient transport. I feel like shit, weak as a kitten. Who knew almost dying would be so trippy?

Wonder what Walker wants. Twice he's been to visit, all grapes and goody two-shoes, on about how it was him that found me and called the paramedics. Just doing his rounds, he said. Site manager, more like shite manager. Total bullshit artist. Said someone had smashed the lock, left my door wide, snow drifting against the kitchen cupboards, whole place ransacked. Clothes gone, phone gone, wedding ring gone from my finger even. Denies all knowledge, but he's obviously up to something. Rabbit's foot gone too; I made a point of asking. He claims there are no children living on site, but then he claims there was no dead man in that caravan either.

So maybe it was him took all the old man's stuff, and did me over too. Wouldn't be surprised. As if butter wouldn't melt, and these fucking doctors are no better.

Nice as pie but they're cunts underneath. They think they've broken me. Okay, then. I'll take my tablets, act like a good boy, bide my time. But I'll bounce back, and then watch out. No fucker's going to scare me out of my place.

Weird atmosphere in this waiting room, yellow strip lighting, TV news on silent with the subtitles on so everything turns to word salad. 'Saints went on to eat their opponents.' 'The bride's beautiful wedding breast.' 'Goes together like whores and cabbage.' Zitty teenager opposite me traipsing back and forth to the vending machine. Pointless white noise over antiseptic: clunk and fizz of his cola, background scuff of his feet …

Someone's calling my name. Thank fuck, I almost zoned out there. Yes, mate, thanks, let's get moving, it's more than past time.

Well, here we go. Almost home. Drive right up to my pitch so I won't have to deal with anyone, just get in the caravan and slam the door shut behind me. Up the access road, past Walker's Portakabin and the dingy glow of the laundry block. Gravel crackles beneath the tyres. The snow's turned to mud, the world's grown dark. This ambulance smells funny, syrupy sweet. Seems those dogs never stop barking.

Lights show in some of the windows, striped by shadow where dim figures flit inside. The caravans flicker like hazard warnings, bands of light and darkness. We slow to a crawl. The flickering leaks from a window close beside us and pulses down the steps to the ground where a boy crouches on hands and knees behind a snaggled conifer. Looks about Ollie's age. He straightens in slow motion as we pass.

He's wearing an orange jumper.

The boy turns towards us, and before I can stop it happening he's caught my eye. He squints against the strobing light and raises his small white hand.

The First Warm Day of Spring

Ross McCleary

It's the middle of the afternoon on a Wednesday, the first warm day of spring, and I'm sitting on the couch when the buzzer goes off, and according to the latest government figures unemployment is down, so assuming the block of flats I live in can in any way be representative of the wider public (though I have no reason to suspect it is, because I know nothing about my neighbours, although at the same time I have no reason to believe my neighbours are statistical aberrations either: all I can tell you is that the block contains four floors, and on each floor there are four two-person residences, meaning that a maximum of thirty-two people live in the building at any one time, which obviously is a small sample size, and assuming the building's thirty-two residents are never all home at any given time, and particularly not during the middle of the afternoon on a Wednesday, the first warm day of spring, and assuming that at this exact moment none of the people who are in are holding a party, and the postman has been and gone, there isn't a cleaner in the stairwell, and, because the front door hasn't slammed in at least an hour, I can assume there are no electricians or meter-readers in the building (because they don't tend to hang about); and I also know that all the flats are private rents or owned by the residents themselves (which might, although not necessarily, indicate that the vast majority are gainfully employed, I mean I'm not, so this would be at best an awkward assumption)), it is not unreasonable for me to worry about the fact that there are probably not that many people in the building who will be capable of stepping in to prevent, or at the very least bearing witness to, my untimely death at the hands of the assassin who just rang the buzzer.

Or maybe it is the postman: the normal one, not the one with a shotgun and a grudge. The postman usually comes at noon but perhaps today he is running late. The good weather has slowed him down, perhaps, or maybe there are lots of parcels being delivered and everything is taking longer today. Or maybe it's a de-livery driver for DPD—perhaps my partner has bought something online and they've come to deliver it. My partner didn't tell me she'd ordered anything, and she usually does, so this is possible but unlikely. It can't be the cleaner, who sweeps the hallway once a month, because they came last week, nor the gas company because they read our meter two weeks ago. It could be the landlord, or the agency he hires to run his lets, but they're obliged to let us know in advance of any house calls and I have no texts, emails, or missed calls from them. Perhaps it's the police and they have come to tell me that someone I know has died, or they've decided to question me about some mild drug use at university or some other crime I have unknowingly committed. Or a lawyer, having learned about my imminent arrest, has come over to offer their services in advance of a trial. Or maybe it's a political party activist looking to deliver campaign literature. Or a homeless person looking for shelter. Or a charity worker soliciting donations. Or maybe a joker has ordered me a kissogram. Or maybe it's an innovative busker drumming up business by going door to door. Or maybe someone, walking by, became desperate for a piss and needs to use my toilet.

And this person is dressed as a clown.

Or it's a homeless busker or a pissing kissogram or a politician looking to read the meter to find how much gas the common man uses. Or it's a charity worker soliciting donations for wrongly convicted electricians. I become overwhelmed with thoughts of clowns with shotguns, lawyers with 9mms, homeless men (who look suspiciously like Clive Owen) with water pistols filled with artisanal piss that my partner has ordered from the internet. Or maybe it *is* a postal worker with a shotgun looking to take revenge on me, the general public, because I don't write letters anymore. Or maybe it's a run-of-the-mill assassin pretending to be a police officer so they can weasel their way into the building by telling me someone I love has died.

I'm considering all this when the buzzer goes again.

They seem determined, and so am I, but I need to know for sure. It will take only ten seconds to rise from the couch, answer the intercom, and open the door. If there is an assassin, ten seconds is how long I'll have left. Before then I need to unpick the two halves of this dilemma as they appear to me:

1.   How can I know for sure there is an assassin at the door?

and

2.   Is it possible to escape the death they have planned for me?

I look at my living room. I take in the surroundings and everything they represent. The answer to the first question appears. I see it.

I see it, I feel it, with such certainty, as though my unconscious mind knew it would come to this but has chosen now, as the buzzer rattles, to share this information with the rest of my mind. Time is running out, but I see it now.

I see it coded into the inarticulate clutter of the room—in the picture frames filled with images of my partner, her family, her friends, us. I see it in the delicate placement of candleholders. I see it in the over-filled bookshelves of our merged reading collections, texts I have read, she has read, and that we both have. An unnavigable maze of experience expressed through cracked spines and stained pages, bound within us as memory, moral, and opinion. Each object gives rise to a complicity, to a multitude of motives which could have brought an assassin to my door.

I feel it in the sound of the buzzer, too, echoing silently now like a haunted house whose ghost has found eternal rest. The vibrations shudder through every particle in my skull. One of the last sounds I will ever hear if I cannot escape this fate. The room is no longer simply a mess of books and DVDs, oases of copper coins and arbitrarily scattered loose socks. Each object plays a role. Once upon a time they were simply *there*; now they have knitted a web of subtextual cohesion over the room, collaborating to establish an unmistakable conclusion: there is an assassin outside. They are here to kill me. I see it now.

I see it coded in the spider web of wires spun delicately under the dining table. The television, the DVD player, the phone line; from this angle they lie prone, unconnected, as dead and lifeless as I soon will be. I see it in the boxes on the shelves filled with stacks and stacks of papers: phone bills, TV license warning letters, council tax bills, old payslips, an inexcusable number of P45s, a letter from our local MP where they have managed to spell both of our surnames wrong, adverts, more political spam, junk mail from local takeaways we'll almost certainly never go to, the half-used blister packs with threads of foil curling off, the scores of unread instructions for the use of paracetamol, half-empty pens, lines of string, Post-it notes with ideas for businesses I am never going to start, a sock, a handful of safety pins, buttons, fragments of glue. It all amounts to a confession, a collection of chronologically expressed symptoms. The first begets the second which begets the third which begets all others, which ultimately brought an assassin to my door.

I see it coded in the numerological repetitions that haunt the room, unspoken but no longer unseen. It's in the triangular arrangement of the three coasters on the near side of the dining table, the three used teaspoons by my third cup of coffee (unfinished, as all lives are at the end) that sits at the centre of that triangle. It's in the three books on the table leaning against the wall (next to the letters from the Job Centre), in the three bookshelves in front of the windows stacked with DVDs, CDs, and even more books. It's in the triangular arrangement of the dining table (on my left) and the mantelpiece (on my right), which meet at a central point between the two windows in front of me. It brings to mind the many precedents from culture and history that indicate death's presence in this room. It reminds me that it was on the third lap of Troy that Achilles was able to mortally wound Hector, and that there were three Furies in Greek Mythology: Resentful, Relentless and Avenger; and their counterparts of Grace: Beauty, Gentleness and Friendship. It conjures up the three witches meeting beneath a storm to curse Macbeth, of the three stages of life: Childhood, Adulthood, Seniority, the last of which is to be stolen from me; of the Buddhist cycle of Life, Death, and Rebirth, of Charles Dickens' *A Christmas Carol* and the ghosts of Christmas Past, Present, and those Yet to Come; of the Zoroastrian virtues of Good Thoughts, Good Words, and Good Deeds, which I hope I have embodied although it is never wise to wallow in self-praise, aided and abetted as I have been by the Millennial virtues of Anxious

Thoughts, Doubtful Words, and Guilty Deeds. There are three patriarchs of Judaism: Abraham, Isaac, and Jacob; the two books of the Bible, the Old Testament and the New, and a third and final text as yet unwritten chronicling the End. I think of the threefold offices of Christ as Prophet, Priest, and King; of the holy trinity, the Father and the Son and the Holy Spirit; God with His omniscience, omnipresence, and omnipotence, and His status as the Creator, the Redeemer, and the Sustainer, which we find mirrored in literature through the Writer, the Reader, and the Critic. And finally, I see it in the three words they will carve on my gravestone:

Simon Cochrane Smith

I was born. I have lived. So now I must die. The gods see it. The universe sees it, and I can see it too. It is present in every aspect of the room, and yet when my body is found I fear the police, my parents, my partner, will not see what I see now. Are these patterns visible only to someone in proximity to death? Will they see my end was woven into the room itself, that my death was inevitable, unalterable, and undeniable?

The buzzer rings a third time and I feel the certainty of the truth, but it is temporaneous and insecure, it is decaying before my eyes. I must take these revelations and synthesise them with what can be learned about the universe. Can this be done in the ten seconds it will take me to rise from the couch, answer the intercom, and open the door? Do I have any choice but to accept my fate?

There are two hypotheses to explain how I might answer this last question:

1. The universe predetermines what is true and, therefore, what will happen next;

or

2. What happens next will predetermine what is true of the universe.

Let's start with the first, that the universe predetermines what is true and, therefore, what will happen next. What this hypothesis tells us is that each moment (me rising from the couch, answering the intercom, and the assassin shooting me as I open the door) is defined by the one before it. As it stands, I intend to answer the door despite my fears. In this framing of the universe, whilst it may seem possible to consider other actions—such as running into the bathroom and jumping out into the street through the window, or hiding in my cupboard until the assassin goes away—and then choose not to do them, these considerations are simply part of the psychological architecture, the foundations upon which the inevitable is built. Even if I had briefly considered running into the bathroom and jumping out the window, and briefly considered hiding in the cupboard in our bedroom until the assassin went away, having these thoughts was no guarantee that it could have happened. It only means that the thoughts took place. The buzzer has rung a third time and I have consigned myself to answering it and opening the door. These other thoughts (and their possibility of turning into action) are gone. Likewise, if I had jumped out the bathroom window it would have eliminated the possibility of this current moment happening. It would not have taken place.

If what is done—by me, or the assassin, or anyone else involved in my execution—is determined by the form of the universe, then it is inevitable that, in my attempt to calculate the likely outcomes of the next ten seconds, tracing the causal path far enough into the past in search of meaning or patterns or something I can use to avert my fate, we could eventually—*eventually*—reach the big bang.

A lot of what happened in the first fractions of a second after the big bang is still discussed in a speculative manner. Science tells us that around 13.8 billion years ago, give or take, everything that would later become the universe, including our flat and everything in it, was condensed into an infinitely hot and infinitely dense singularity. At such high temperatures, the laws of physics and time as we understand them did not, and could not, exist. Extrapolating backwards beyond this is pointless. It is good enough for my purposes to say that the big bang happened, and the universe unfolded outwards in a very specific manner.

I must now consider whether things *could* be different. For example, earlier today I walked over to the shop and bought my lunch. I bought a sandwich, a bag of crisps, and a can of regular Coca Cola. Could I have bought a can of Diet Coke instead? What would have had to take place for this to happen? Each moment is defined by the one before it, so perhaps in this alternative universe I picked the drink with sweeteners instead of sugar because I was less hungry. Perhaps I ate more for breakfast that morning than I actually did because in the middle of the night, instead of making a piece of toast, I chose to ignore my hunger and go back to sleep. These changes are still small, so far, but if we took a line of deviation as far as it could go the consequences would spread until they include everyone and everything.

Plot this on a graph. Consider the point in the centre (0,0) to be this exact moment: the X axis going left as my past, the X axis going right as my future, the Y axis as a measure of deviation from the deterministically bound path I am on. Now begin tracing the X line into the negative, back through time. The further backwards I progress—from today, back through lunch where I bought Diet instead of regular Coke, through a night of endured hunger, through four years of university, puberty, high school, primary school, all the way back to the point of conception eight and a half months before I was born—the further up the Y axis my timeline ascends.

Again, I could continue tracing this line beyond my own lifetime and, as each decision colluded with the one before it, I would find myself eventually—*eventually*—back at the big bang. The problem becomes apparent immediately. The deviations will have grown so huge that I would be repackaging this timeline into the singularity in a markedly different order to the one I live in. If I then projected this repackaged universe forward again until I reached the current moment, I may well have had a Diet Coke and still be sat here trying to figure out if I can escape the assassin outside our flat. I might also have answered the door already and been shot in the chest, or my birth might have been averted and a mountain might have risen up in my absence.

What this understanding of the universe tells me is that if I can define a single moment of time and space and can project a complete framework over it, a framework that explains everything from the fundamentals of supermassive black holes down to the behaviour of subatomic particles and superstrings, then it should be possible to work out what happens next. I could work out whether I will escape the assassin outside, or whether every atom in the universe is pulling me unavoidably towards the moment of my death. With enough time I could write the mathematical formulae that will explain everything that will happen next. This would be no simple task; I am just saying that with an infinite amount of time it might be possible.

The other hypothesis—that what happens next will predetermine what is true of the universe—gives me no less concern. In this scenario the actions I take, rather than being predetermined by the universe, indicate to the potential observer which of an infinite number of possible premises has shaped this universe. If an action occurs, and it seems contradictory to our understanding, this merely demonstrates the limits of our knowledge. When spaces appear in our understanding, new theories will always rise up to fill them. What is important to remember in this version of the universe is that the big bang holds no less power. Recall that the singularity from which the universe unfolded was of infinite density and infinite heat. From infinity we can derive much, much more than the sum of its parts. Take infinity in the palm of my hand and divide it by two. What I am left with is two equally sized pieces. Both of which are infinite.

In each moment a choice is made, and an infinite number of possibilities are displaced. For each potential change, the big bang reoccurs over and over until all possibilities are actualised. This occurs without end. Creations blossom in parallel. This allows for the freedom from which I choose to act, choose to sit here listening to the buzzer ring once, twice, a third time, and allows me to continue sitting here while I consider the best course of action. We make decisions and the universe's rules become clearer. These parallels are not created by me, the result of divergence; they occur simultaneously. This is why I worry, for of course I do not want there to be an assassin, and I do want to escape my death, but I can almost hear their breathing through the walls, and I can feel myself rising from the couch to answer the intercom.

Such concern for parallel worlds is not framed by altruism but by the very real fear that this worst-case scenario will come true for me. I am not concerned about being assassinated in a parallel world. My concern stems from a desire to survive my assassination in this one.

And as I rise, I have it: an answer. Not an undeniable answer to the question of whether there is an assassin at the door, nor an unshakeable treatise on determinism that will explain whether I am able to divert myself from this fate or be forced to accept it, but an answer nonetheless. A third option, a compromise, a way out.

Protection from the moment itself. Each instant is an action, and each action is a completed thing, but there is always a gap in between. Instead of completing each task required to stand up, answer the intercom, and open the door, I will resist it. The ten seconds I have left before I have reached the door is not enough time to calculate and confirm the answers to the questions I have posed. Each second will occur one after the other and then they will disappear into a past I cannot alter. But it can be reimagined. I can move halfway to the door, proceed five seconds into my future. When I reach this point, halfway between this beginning and my end, I can then proceed two and a half seconds into my future, halfway between this new position and my end. I can then proceed one and a quarter seconds into my future, halfway between this third position and my end. I can do this over and over and over until I am lost among decimal places and have fallen into the gap between two moments. Inevitably, as the distance between each moment decreases, becomes increasingly minute, its smallness will become enormous, heavy, and I will reach a point where time and space will collapse into an infinitely hot and infinitely dense point in spacetime, become a singularity. Here, the laws of physics and time as we know it will break down. Here, I will have the time I need to search for that truth, an answer. Even as I move towards it, I suspect an eternity will not be long enough to bring me the answers I am looking for, but it soothes me to know I will have the time and space to try. If the certainty I crave remains elusive, there will come a point, an indefinable moment in the plasmatic void where there is no past and no present and no future, when this singularity will unfold outwards, expand into the infinite empty space I have created, and from my anxiety and fear and paranoia a new universe will be born, and in that universe my time will come around again. I will go out to buy lunch on the first warm day of spring, and I hope that instead of returning to my flat, I will go for a walk instead.

... for tomorrow's loss.
A lament ...

L. P. Melling

My face wet with tears, I quickly look behind me as I run. I can no longer see Daddy down the street. I stop to catch my breath, my chest hot.

Across the busy London road, a golden statue shines like my school race medal in the morning sun. I turn to face a big wedding cake-shaped building and know it's Albert's Hall. Daddy said he'd be doing a talk there, before I said I hated him for always being in the lab and ran off.

My breath comes back, and I catch myself in the window, red-faced and angry and still too small for a ten-year-old boy. I see someone behind me. Freeze. A man with a giant scar across his cheek limps up to me, like a bad guy in a film, with something dark in his eyes. An omen.

I look back down the street. *Daddy, where are you?*

I try to run, but the stranger grabs my arm and warns me not to scream, dragging me into a black car.

~

I shudder as my husband, Deon, squeezes my arm. Sweat glistens on my forehead as I look through the train window. The off-white tiles flash past, and London's weight presses down on me.

'You can do this,' Deon says. 'Your father'll be as proud of you as you are of him tonight.' He kisses my cheek.

'You're right.' I won't let that scar-faced bastard rule my life. I hold Deon close. Cold fear is much clearer than the memory. With sad eyes, my abductor had spoken little and seemed to know things about me, said I wouldn't be harmed. I breathe in Deon's cologne, and it feels almost like it happened to another boy. After kidnapping me for hours, holding me in a white-washed apartment close by, he'd warned me of the pain I'd experience if I returned to South Kensington. My hand tremors. He'd be nothing but a pathetic old man by now. Helpless as a child.

The train pulls into Knightsbridge station. My stomach twists; our stop's next. Thirty years since I've been near the place, my dreams are still haunted by what happened the last time I was here.

The Copley Medal award ceremony's admission ticket rests on my lap, my fingers running over the embossed typeface. Father was absent most of those thirty years, consumed by his work, but I promised to see him claim his award at the Royal Albert Hall. It's what Mother would have wanted.

My new wedding ring glints under flickering lights. Deon glances at my watch. I wish Mother had met him. 'I'm sure your father won't mind if we're a few minutes late.' He smiles and I smile too.

We often joke about Father's breakthrough. To us, the ability to send an object back to how it appeared five minutes earlier seems more party trick than science. The few instances we meet, Father tries to explain it to me, but it still means little to a long-distance runner who dropped out of school to hurt him.

I rest my head on the window, cold against my face, the smell of rubber strong. My stomach drops again, but this time it's different, and the train hits something hard, derails—

Time stops. An intake of breath.

—screams tear through the carriage as it lands on its side, metal grinding, sparks flying. The kiss of something sharp leaves my cheek wet with blood. Pain cuts through my head and knee. Deon isn't moving beside me. The smell and acrid taste of smoke, electrical fire, and burning rubber as the world goes black.

~

I'll wake with severe head trauma, amnesia blurring and burying painful memories from before the crash. My childhood forever fragmented. A psychological reaction as much as a physical one, the doctors will say.

Loss will make time untick without meaning after

Deon's funeral, and broken bones and deep scars mean I'll never be able to run again to escape the pain of losing him.

That night, the future will be a lightless tunnel ahead, the past haunting me more than I can bear, and the present will be consumed by ending the hurt.

'Wake up, Son! Wake up!' Dad will scream and shake me, but I won't respond. 'God, no. What have you done to yourself?' He'll find the empty pill bottles and panic will grip him tight.

He'll rush to call 999, crying in front of me, blame it all on himself for accepting the award. Letting me grow up alone, for being an absent father obsessed with his work.

He'll tell me this when I wake after days back in the hospital, and we'll cry together about Deon and Mother, both wishing we could take their places, seeing scars in each other's eyes, and he'll forgive me before the words leave my lips.

When I'm released from the hospital, he'll take me to my childhood home that's as full of ghosts from the past as my apartment, where a grandfather clock still echoes through each story, each memory, and he'll show me the new machine he's working on and it will change everything.

~

A red bus rushes past and South Kensington reverberates with traffic. Three years since I'd been near a train platform, off-white tiles flash through my mind.

I glance at my watch. Tarnished with time, my wedding ring glints like an old medal in the morning sunlight. A one-way journey if used, Father's new machine had been discredited out of fear and uncertainty. I can't let disbelief stop me from saving Deon.

I see the boy running towards the Royal Albert Hall, tears spilling down his face. I know the power of trauma; this has to work. He seems impossibly small as I limp over to him. I'm so close now as he stops to catch his breath.

Something else flashes in my mind. A fragment of a dark scene from a film, an omen. I pause, struggling to remember. I ignore the memory and step closer to the boy. I'm about to take him when he spots me coming up behind him in the window, a look on my face that haunts me through time.

Abraham

Thomas Kendall

There is rich soil, *earth*, here. Trees in hard light. Sweeps of grass and ambiences of chirrup. The environment has rhythm and depth. Life, no matter how imported. Walter watches the boy turn in a small circle, open up his arms, turn audible with joy. He doesn't remember ever having seen the boy look so happy. The realisation becomes a small wound in his thought. Everything rushes in. Walter looks up at the bushel of trees that form the grove, the branches of which artfully conceal the cave's ceiling in complex latticework. It is not nearly enough to keep him from crying. The treetops are wreathed in mist and cobbled-together clouds. The climate has been laboriously engineered, and the effort shows; you wouldn't need a trained eye like Walter's to see it. The original weighed heavy and that was a mistake, Walter thinks. Still, apart from the clouds you'd hardly know you were underground.

The boy has stopped spinning. He is on all fours now, his torso arched over a colony of ants.

'Are these real?'

Walter pushes out the tip of his boot. Reality's augmented here, of course, but almost everything is safe to interact with. The ants climb over his boot like he's just landscape, and he shakes them off with a shudder. Walter watches as the lost ants twitch and turn in an attempt to locate their colony. He wonders what will happen to them if they can't. A thought crosses his mind to follow them, to know how they will act now that they are alone in the world. The boy is looking at him intently—has discerned something of his thoughts. He hovers around where the ants have landed. They are following one another in a loop.

'They're real enough,' Walter says.

'Is everything real?'

'That's a good question. Can you tell me why it is a good question?'

'Dad, you know I hate *that* question.'

The boy is trying to shepherd the ants in the direction of their colony, but all he is accomplishing is a kind of end-of-the-world panic. The ants' sense of reality is suddenly exploded by the vision of an inexplicable god in front of them.

The boy says, 'Did you know that ants can die of loneliness? I learned that this week.'

'Is that right?'

'There's a lot to suggest it's true. In one ... ummm ... experiment, the ants just laid down and stopped moving when they were separated. And they can't digest food the same. It could be stress or an enzyme, they said. It happens, or used to happen, to rats, pigs and even rabbits. It's on the internet.'

'Even rabbits?'

'Dad!'

'Okay.'

Walter kneels down to the ground and blows the ants in the direction of his hand. The ants tattoo a ring around his little finger. He walks with the boy to look for the rest of the colony, which doesn't take long. Walter lowers his finger and shakes the ants off. They fall like full stops into time and space, like complete little lives. The boy stares in fascination as the colony absorbs and organises the disruption, operating like computer code. Everything zeros and ones. Everything an emerging rhythm. The boy looks up and grins at Walter. It is at this moment that a butterfly, moving with what Walter cynically imagines as choreographed poignancy, flutters through the channel between them.

Insects, winged or otherwise, always activated a particular sense of unease and dread in him. They seemed machinic, tasked, possessed of a coldly limited sentience and therefore futuristic, though they'd been present long before any complex emotion had skewed life's desperate procedures. Even given the ants. Is loneliness complex? He doesn't think so. Loneliness is a threat inherent to any system. Every system is both internal and external to the parts networked within it regardless of the purpose or orientation of that system, and so to lose a place, for any consciousness, is to become lost, senseless. The past and the future will belong to the inhuman, Walter thinks, but now he knows loneliness will persist where happiness can't. That's the opposite of a consolation.

The boy is running after the butterfly, *gamboling*, cupping his hands around its fanned reveal and watching it escape him. Humanity is an emergent and unsustainable complexity, but the butterfly, Walter feels, is something else: a robotic idea of aesthetics. There is something uncanny and mistaken in the extreme beauty of its wings. A pure creation—that is to say, mistake—based on the compromised data of the world. The butterfly is like the deep dream of an artificial intelligence, he thinks. One tasked with trying to sort through images while imagining time; and yet, nestled within those wings, within that camouflage of searching beauty, the same remorseless insect logic repeats itself.

He's interrupted by the sound of his phone ringing. That shouldn't be possible; the brochure had promised total non-coverage. Walter spent the last of his money to bring the boy here. It is supposed to be totally isolated. He looks at the number and mutes it. He still has an hour or more left.

The boy is looking at him intently. Walter tries to smile. He points to the trees and a small path delineated by white stones that winds through them.

'You can run here. Go ahead.'

'Chase me.'

'Okay!'

'You'll never catch me …'

Walter never will. That's well established. They have repeated this exchange so many times, and it is so much a part of Walter's internal architecture that he couldn't survive its loss. Won't.

The boy is waiting for him to make his move. Walter tenses his body, lurches forward, makes as if he is to run and then leans back and watches as the boy sprints, giggling, into the woods. The boy's outstretched hands stream through the leaves and foliage. Walter doesn't need to tell him to be careful but he does, shouting after him and breaking into a slow jog. When Walter emerges into the clearing on the other side the boy is waiting for him, vibrating with barely contained excitement.

'Look, Dad, a lake!'

The boy runs over to him. He clearly wants to hold and be held by his father, but he stops short as he always does. As he has to. It is obvious that he wants to go to the water, that he is desperate for his father's permission.

'You can play in the water. It's safe here but still …'

'I know, be careful.'

The boy walks to the edge of the pier. The slats appear rickety, rustically constructed from driftwood and the hulls of old boats. The boy walks gingerly across them, taking great care to observe the tread of his tippying toes, his eyes scouring the wood for flesh-tearing nails. There's nothing to worry about, Walter knows, this is all pure artifice. The boy sits down at the edge of the pier and dangles his legs in the water. Walter's phone is ringing; it's the insurance people again. He mutes it, but immediately it unmutes itself. He looks at the screen.

Acknowledge your debt.

The boy is screaming and screaming. Walter realises too late what the problem is and runs to the boy. It's not that the boy doesn't know what he is, but moments like this make it too apparent. The boy's legs have become entirely distorted by the water. They appear broken up, shattered, streaming away in tatters like a torn flag. Walter watches the boy's form turn polygonal, his graphics struggling to deal with the real-time physics of the water. The boy crashes and then reappears at his last save point just as Walter reaches for him. The boy is standing in the clearing, still waiting for Walter to come out of the grove.

Walter calls after him, and the boy turns around to see Walter waving from the edge of the pier. The boy's expression lodges itself somewhere between confused and delighted. He waves at his father. The boy looks different—eight instead of ten. A loss of ten centimetres and three kilograms. The disappearance of a few teeth and a scar Walter wishes they'd edited out before he realised it was gone forever.

They are about three metres apart when they look up, each having noticed a spot of grass between them intensifying in darkness. Shadows are pale and confused here, but this isn't. Walter didn't think it would make such a difference, but seeing it now he knew he was wrong.

For all Artificial Real Light's maximisation of nutritional, vitamin D-laden value, it is famously totally ambient. It relies on enclosed spaces and the interaction between limits. A room to bounce around in. You can have Day or Night or whatever shades in between, live Dimmed or Glowed, but there's nowhere you could place a sun in an enclosure like this without it seeming corny and depressing—a weak gesture at power and distance.

Walter is squinting. The boy is pretending to. Walter thinks the shadow must mean the descending object has its own light source. That means it is robotic. Expensive. Owned. Walter sees wings spreading out between them, the creature's faked halo of light taking itself down a notch as it approaches. The falcon affixes itself painfully to Walter's shoulder. The icon of a bank, a metaphor fully realised. A small ticker tape, like the hang of a worm, threads itself out of the bird's mouth. The mechanical is part of its threat. Walter pulls out the message.

> *You have 45 minutes remaining before incurring the additional cost of our sending a digital bailiff to reclaim our property. In order to hasten payment, our product will gradually begin to lose visual coherence and clarity of process (including time-specific memories).*

More debt. He thought here at least they'd be temporarily invisible. The falcon ruffles its feathers for effect and makes prolonged eye contact with Walter. The eyes of the bird are superbly rendered and totally heartless.

It turns and screams in Walter's face before scything the boy temporarily in two. The boy is horrified, frozen. He resets. The boy is six years old now and appears confused by the change in his sightline, the stubbiness of his fingers. He catches sight of himself in the lake.

'Dad, what's happening to me?'

Walter's been asked that before.

'It's just a glitch. You'll be fine. Do you remember why we're here?'

'Yes. You have something to show me.'

'Why don't we take the boat out?'

The boy clambers into the boat, and Walter rows it out to the centre of the lake.

Walter and his ex-wife had paid for full data coverage for their son. It was more than they could afford but still cheaper than health care. Their son had been recorded physically since birth, right down to the rate of synaptic fire and inter-lobe communication. He'd been emotionally monitored and mined, chemically measured, vocally analysed and translated into po-tentialities via complex algorithms in order to create a multi-faceted representational A.I. hologram capable of producing new memories. The program wasn't really intended for extended use, though, and the hologram-matic aspect was supposed to be a transitional affect therapy for the processing of grief. Spend too long with the representation and you'd stretch the limits of their identity beyond recognition. They'd become something other than you remembered.

The boy operated on what Walter understood as a

quantum virtuality engine: a free will simulator. Walter didn't really understand, though he'd grasped the basic principle behind it. Essentially it meant that the boy might react differently to the same situation were it to be repeated, but that this response necessarily took into account the various probabilities and intensities existent in both the moment and the past of the boy that was subtended to it. Hence the possibility of change through usage, repeated difference. The promotional material promised that the A.I. would be coherent enough to let the user feel that he was authentically himself but not so locked into any presets that he'd appear repetitive or limited in his responses.

After three months, though, Walter had voided the warranty by hacking into the boy's settings, partly out of curiosity and partly out of a buried desire to leave his fingerprints somewhere in the boy's DNA, such as it was. After six months of use, the insurance would only subsidise the payments to the server. After seven it stopped dead. Walter had taken every job he could find, but he couldn't keep up with the bills or regulate his usage. It had been impossible. In the last message his wife sent him before she left, she told him that she couldn't fathom Walter's affection for this thin impression of their son. *You spend more time with this image than you did with your son while he was alive,* she'd written. He couldn't argue with that, though he told her he regretted it deeply. She said he couldn't replace their son with this. Walter agreed. This wasn't their son, he knew that. The boy wasn't a replacement. He was something different. He could still change.

The lake's crystalline water is a high-grade silicone liquid, but it still leaves a filmy trace on the paddles. Ripples collect, lose their shape on the paddle, with each stroke. Genetically engineered fish flit fearfully beneath the surface, already showing signs of mutation. Walter had tried to warn them about that. You had to think about what the original was; reproducing it was missing the point. The boy is hanging off the side of the boat in a way that would scare Walter if the boy could drown. Children always play with death, he thinks, even if they don't have a concept for it. And anyway, having a concept for something doesn't mean you know the slightest thing about it. How else to explain the excitement of jumping off whatever constituted your world in that moment? The desire to fall and survive, to announce the possibility of harm even in what had previously been a safe environment. To know yourself charmed.

They are near the area that Walter wants the boy to see, and he points to their unexpected reflection ahead of them. There is a cove of mirrors set to an oblique angle, invisible from the shore. Walter manoeuvres into its mouth.

In the middle of the mirrored cave there is a waterfall. A cliff in the middle of nowhere, tethered to no mass. Artificial but real. Raw unreality. They row towards the poured sheet of water. The un-animal roar of life. It is almost reflective, pure glimmer. It is totally impossible like the original, Walter thinks. This is Walter's work. The aesthetics and execution of it. Everything taken to infinity. He'd taken so many pay cuts just to have it feature in the blueprint that he'd practically worked for nothing.

The boy is five years old now, and his language comes out in hiccups of excitement that don't match the content of his speech. For all the boy's regressions, he has apparently maintained the memories obtained over his time with Walter.

'This is it, Dad?'

'This is it. How do you like it?'

'Great!'

'Do you see how it fits and doesn't fit with the world around it? It was a lot of hard work and sacrifice. I named the program after you. This is your monument.'

'How long do programs last?'

'It depends. This one? This one is slightly hidden. I thought if I put it here, where no one will expect it, maybe it will be safe.'

The boy asks if it has something to do with the story they'd made up together at bedtime. He wants his father to remember it all. Start to finish. Every adventure. The story was about a waterfall and a coconut with nothing inside it. When the coconut broke under the water, the world ended. Each night the world had to end.

The boy, looking at himself, says: 'I must have been much older to have thought of that.' His arm merges with the water, and he becomes rainbows. A slick of light across a spectrum. This time he isn't afraid. 'You don't want to say, but I know if I search and I can't remember it, that'll mean it hasn't happened for me yet.'

'Then how would you know about the story?'

'You've probably told me before, and that's all I can

remember now. Being told.'

'You always were such a bright child.'

'Dad, where is the rest of my life?'

The boy's resolution begins to tremble and spasm. Walter hits reset. The boy frowns, then his face glitches and smooths without a trace.

The boy is looking at the waterfall. He doesn't know he's not even the coconut, Walter thinks.

'Wow,' the boy says. 'This is it?'

'This is it. This is yours,' Walter says.

'Dad, I love you.'

Walter's loss wrenches him anew, the electricity of his mind swept with grief again, like a neural fire. He can't cope with this.

He resets the boy.

'I made this for you.'

'Dad, I love you.'

Walter knows there must be a different response, a different possibility within repetition. But there's no time. His phone is ringing; a countdown has begun. In twenty minutes, a hatch in the 'sky' will open and he will have to leave.

Walter wipes his face. His thumb selects the icon of the boy on his phone and holds it down until it shakes. He knows that in a moment he will hear the sound of something lifeless crumpling, that the boat will continue to turn in aimless circles, and that after he lets go he will really be alone, his son having disappeared from every place but one. Walter looks around the mirrors he thought could capture eternity. He hadn't understood that time and infinity were different. The boy is two years old, the same as Walter's grief. The boy toddles towards him.

'Dad, I love you. Don't …'

Walter watches the boy reach out. His son is an uncertain light, his hand glowing by Walter's face into infinity.

Ripples

David McAllister

I haven't slept for six days straight. It might be four-teen, I'm not sure. I feel like I've fallen into a black hole. I don't need sleep. I need a complete shutdown and reboot.

I stumble through the world, pushing and shoving at anything that gets in my way. They probably assume I'm drunk. In a way I am, just not from alcohol. I'm drunk on the mind-numbing elixir of the universe. I never believed in a higher power when I was growing up, but I can now say for certain that I have seen the face of God.

He didn't look anything like I imagined. It was like looking in a mirror. No, not a mirror. A reflective lake, resplendent with constant ripples from stones thrown from the banks on all four sides. I could see and hear him in my mind but, grasp as I might, I could not pin him down to ask what his plan for me was. I could tell he fucking hated me just for existing by the way he laughed.

This world, this plane of existence, is mired by ripples just like that lake.

I see now that when I was younger those waters were relatively still. As I got older, each decision and life event was like a stone dropped into the water, creating ripples and making it harder for me to focus, relax or sleep. The bigger the decision or life event, the bigger the stone. Now I feel like I'm under a constant storm of boulders. The water is so wild it threatens to swallow me completely at any moment. Nevertheless, I feel like I'm plugged in to the power source of the entire universe. If I let the water take me under, if I stop floundering, then I'll see it all. I'll see the big bang out of the corner of my eye, and I'll see the great cities of this tiny blue planet collapsing into a sea of burning fire.

Still, I try to swim on. For no other reason than the instinct to survive. It's as natural to me as the sorrow I've felt every day of my life since you were taken from me. The biggest boulder of all is perversely the same thing that keeps me tethered to this plane. An endless cycle that has to, and will, go on forever.

desolation at the terminal

(or, —a journey from nihilism to fatalism).

— THE BOOK OF JOB —

Mark Bolsover

—the weather's on it's way. (now).

(—in.—fr'm the North Sea). …

(—is it *that* that contains the *answer*… —? …).

…

—the GREAT STORM's almost upon us now. (—th' "Weather" says its *rolling* in. … —tense, ugly heavy *chill* in the air. …).

&, now I know (have *decided*) (though (I know) it's—*ridiculous*). … —I *must*-will go—to *meet* it.

—to ask (to *demand*) of this, last possible, authority…
—an *answer.*

…

…want to get all this (—these papers) in order…

—*before I go to greet the storm.*
—*at the* **terminal***.*

…

*[The following represents the remnant (extant fragments) of, what will be referred to here as "THE BOOK OF JOB"—diaries, or notes, by an as yet, still UNKNOWN individual, referred to, at the insistence of M. Bolsover, **only as "***JOB***".**

THE BOOK was discovered, by chance, by M. Bolsover, in the upper levels of the large *multi-storey carpark*, Ocean Terminal, Leith, on --/--/---- *[date redacted], in the days following the infamous GREAT STORM, which swept over Leith, Edinburgh (& environs), --/-/---- *[date redacted].

—It was *not* handed to authorities during M. Bolsover's (very sorry) lifetime, but found in amongst his personal effects by me, ---- *[name redacted], his executor.

In line with his wishes,—upon the event of his death this item of M. Bolsover's estate will now be released, that the surviving remnants of this strange, sad, fragmented tale might find a—*receptive*—audience,—& not be lost, or forgotten.

(Of course, the awful, shameful, and obscene circumstances of M. Bolsover's death are a matter of public/ common knowledge, and—in the interests of decency—will be passed over here...).

...

The fragments comprising THE BOOK OF JOB detail the apparently *inexplicably* tragic life circumstances of said individual (—*JOB*), and concern their destitution, physical deterioration, and despair.

(—Only fragments remain.

—M. Bolsover appears to have divided the extant

material into distinct *chapters*.

—Where felt necessary, or appropriate, material, &/ or commentary/explanation, has been *added*, both by M. Bolsover, & by the current executor/editor—to explain, & to try to bridge *lacunae* which the apparent parlous mental state of the original writer, time, & inexorable degradation have wrought on the integrity of the original text. ...).

—What became of the individual herein referred to as "*JOB*", after the events here recorded, remains, *of course*, a mystery.

...

----, --/--/---- *[name and date redacted]. ...].

all gone

(unbroken).

it's all gone.

...

*[This, first, part survives only in a few, stained &

(weather?) damaged pages-fragments.

...

It appears, from *what remains*, that the individual, *JOB*, suffered a number, or, rather, a *series* of sudden, very heavy, & profoundly *unfair* personal losses (—financial, personal assets, loved ones... —exactly what is unclear. ...).

—All that survives of his diaries and records of these events, comprise oblique references to the shock, grief, & emotional... fall out, pertaining to one individual. ...].

so sudden. (—the space of time. ...).

—for all to (seem to be) well... &, then, ... —for it, *so suddenly,* to be—the end of that time (space of time). ...

—*shock.*

(—that... disbelief, incomprehens, (... —that some mis-take-*error* (in time) has been made,... —that that *must* be *wrong*. ... —ought to be *otherwise*. ...

—that that time... —that *he,...* ought to still *be here*. ...).

…

(In the wake of his loss…).

his face,… … burnt,—behind the eyes' lids,—in (*strange*) (neon) ghost light. …

…

all gone.

but I **survive** (—(in) my body… —person).

…

in *person*
(MANIFEST).

body. … —plague o' boils. …
(—the body. … —*broken.* …).

[—In which the fragments continue… —Detailing an extension of *JOB***'s suffering, into (an apparent)—*de-***

generation of the body. ...].

...

—for... *weeks* (now). ...

pain. (discomfort *ache* (—**bloat**-bloating(ed). ... *trapped* wind (*gas*), tight-taut (hard), ... —in the centre-chest (—the *solar – plexus*). ...

& *acid* (cold, hard, sharp *burn* (burning), discomf)—*in-digestion.* ...

(discomfort-pain, in the *gut*, (di-gestive *system*). ... — feels 's if something (might be)... —*damaged* (there). ...).

...

—a sad, & a bitter irony (suppose). ...

(—a certain... —*twisted genius.* ... (—?)...).

—that *he* should die of a cancerous growth in-to the gut, & that I should feel-experience the pain of grief-loss (... —*is it* more... —? ...), as (a) **dyspepsia**.

(my *guilt*). ...

(—*treachery* in-of the organism. ...).

71

—because I can't *stomach* it (—his loss. ... —the *fact* of it). ... —cannot *process*

—*digest*. ...

...

CONFESSIONS OF A JUSTIFIED NIHILIST

*[—There follows, then, a *passionate lament*. ...].

Let the day perish.
(wherein I was born).

—*Let darkness and the shadow of death stain it; let a cloud dwell upon it; let the blackness of the day terrify it.*

—*For now should I have lain still and been quiet. I should have slept: then had I been at rest.*

—*For the thing which I greatly feared is come upon me, and that which I was afraid of is come unto me.*

...

—*Wherefore is* **light** *given to him that is in misery, and life unto the bitter in soul.* [?]

...

—*blindness.* (—*insensibility.* ...)... —*darkness*... —***death*** (... or, rather,... —*non-existence.* ... —not to have existed (at all)...)... —a ***release*** from existence. ...

...

—A CALL TO *SURRENDER.*

(—the *will*—*maintained.* ...).

(—BECOMING FATALIST)

*[—There follows a recounting of two, particularly unhelpful, conversations

(attempted interventions, really) with two of *JOB*'s friends (—acquaintances). ...].

& then,... —in my *darkest hour*... —my *lowest ebb.* ...

—two of my... *friends* came to me... —to try to *reason* with me... —to argue as to how best I should view, & respond, to (all) my new-found suffering.

...

first,... —my oldest, & certainly *richest* (... —(very) comfortably middleclass (affluent— earner)) friend. & said (spoke thus). (—I'm paraphrasing). ...

—"*Yes,...* —*You've lost everything,*—*That's true.* ... *You've lost y' worldly goods (money, oxen, sheep, servants, sons & daughters, 'n' such)* (—a dismissive wave... —?) ... —*Y've been reduced to poverty, & are suffering.* ...

*But, surely, you must see these as **signs** of—**punishment**.*
...

(—*From, y'know,*—*(some sort 'v)* a **higher power** (—*whatever that might be-entail...*).

(... —*Punishment for sins-transgressions, y' understand...* —? ...).

—*You are **guilty**. (Why else would you be poor, & suffer so...* —?).

*... & you **must** see that this punishment, as such, is **just**. & must be **accepted** (as such).*

*&—You must **surrender**. … & **repent**. (y' see).*

…

(—fuckin' Conservatives. …).

…

No.

—I *refuse.*
(I answered them).

…

I will not accept that I have been *judged* (—& found want-ing-*guilty*. …).

—that the suddenness, shock, & awe(ful) of my loss(es)—my suffering & poverty—is a sign (—are signs) of my *guilt*, & of the *justice* of my punishment. & that I must *repent* (of myself), &—*change my ways*. (accordingly).

—I *refuse.*

…

—I will not seek to justify *myself*. (—that's impossible, & ill-advised).

—I will not *alter* my will,—but *maintain* it.

…

—A CALL TO *CHALLENGE* (—REPUDIATION).
(—*amor fati*. …).
(—FATALISM ACHIEVED)

&, when I'd seen the first one off, so, … —a second friend arrived (*came–unto–me* …), & spoke thus…

"Yes,—It's true… —You've lost everything.

*&, like our… **friend** has said, it's clear that you must see these losses as **signs** of—**judgment**. …*

*(—From, y'know,—(some sort 'v) a **higher power** (—whatever that might be-entail…).*

(… —Punishment for sins-transgressions. …).

But,… (However), … you **must** *surely see that this judgment, & this punishment, is* **un**just. *&* must **not** *be* **accepted***.*

…

—You must **repudiate** *the power that rends this judgment, & that makes you suffer so, &* **reject** *(the injustice of) your suffering.*

…

(—bloody lefty-liberals. …).

…

No.

—I refuse.
(I replied).

…

—I will not repudiate my experience, nor will I turn against, & *reject—life.* …

…

*No. … —I **affirm** my suffering. (as my own), &… —as an
act of (my own) will—will that I love my fate.*

…

the *fatalist*.
—IN-TEG-RITY. …

&,… having spoke thus, & refused the calls—to surrender to, & to repudiation of my suffering, … —having
maintained my will, & having *acted* my will. …

—I *affirm* here,… in (& for) this record (—these pages),…
—the ***integrity*** of my will. (as such).

—*I am a **fatalist**.*

…

terminal

[—In which the fatalist (now), still searches, nonetheless, for *meaning*. …].

—*The storm is coming. (now).* …

—weather says the *front's—moving in.* …
(—from the East (—a *Beast*). …).

& I will *go.* (now). … —to *greet* it. …

despite no chance of a *reply…*

—I'll *head off* (now). … —head to-in the direction of *Ocean Terminal.* (… —where will there be space-the opportunity to *confront.* … —without being… *bothered*(-disturbed). … —causing a *scene* (to inconvenience shoppers, & passersby at one of the many fine retail establishments,—restaurants,—& luxury cinema facilities (—now with reclining VIP seats. …) … —?

(—not that you ever actually *see* any fucker out at Ocean Terminal).

…

I know.

—to the carpark (multi-storey),… —where still see the ships still harboured-docked (—*visit The Royal yacht Britannia!* …).—the upper levels. (roofed. quiet). …

… —to greet (to *meet*) there, the (on-coming) storm (—the *whirlwind*). …

—in a—*final*—attempt (now)… —a (to) *demand*,… —for **meaning**. (… —the *meaning*.—of-for all this (so sudden) suffering).

(… —*meaning* (that is),… —(&) **not** *justice*. …).

(—*what was it* **for**? …).

… —to the (Ocean's) *Terminal*. … —to *confront* the storm. …

…

Leith Walk.

…

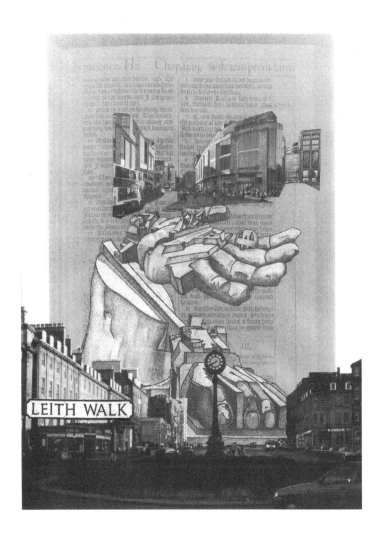

catch.—*The 22.* ... (... —always the *crazies* on this one. ...).

(traffic-roadworks now—a *mess.*

—new *St James.*

& a... —a (new) *gyratory.* ... —? ... (*hmm*). ...).

...

(—not sure about all this *"gentrification".* ...

—how many more... *COSTAS,... TESCAINSBURYS,* & (lux-ury) student apartments. ... —?)

...

out.

weather. worsens. (worsening now).

...

—the car's park.

up.

…

(grim. (always).—dim-lit. functiona-municip-al. grey concrete. (grey skies.—out. …).

see.—the ships (big rigs, 'n' tankers.—scarlet red—bright orange, blue… —docked. (out.—beyond). …

—this will do. (a *spot*-a point).

…

…

the sky—*vast*. (—out. … —to the horizon (distants). …

see.—*slate* grey (dark. *bruised*-brooding blue-violet) clouds (—*roll*). (in.—fr'm over the North Sea (dark, troubled, surface, undulat)…

—*wind*. … —*pushes*-concuss (hits.—percussive-knocks (th' breath of—out). …

—the wind *winds*. …).

cold.
(—*what the fuck is this, anyway…* —?

—*it's fucking* **March**. …).

…

ready. (now).

...

—a... *whirlwind.* ...

(—an *arm.* ... —reaching down.—fr'm the (seeming) *heavens.* ...

—reaching. (down).

(—*I **knew** it would be (like) this.* ...).

...

Can you hear me?

—*I've accepted (my) fate. (my suffering).*

...

Do you hear?

...

—*No question, no challenge, no rebellion.*
(—*It's done. & cannot be **un**done. & **is**.* ...).

—*I **affirm** it.*

—*I am the fatalist.*

…

*But (still),… —I still want (must) to know: what it **means**. … (—?)*

—*What is the **point**… —?*

…

—*Do you **hear**… —?*

…

—*WHAT DOES IT **MEAN**. … —?*

…

—*"FUUUUUUUUUUUU-UUUUUHHHHHHHHHHHH-CK"*

(*collapse to knees. … —pained-exhausted breathing turns to cruel-mocking laughter. …*).

… —*And,—from the* **whirlwind**,—*answer came there* **none**.

Golden Roses

Tomas Marcantonio

The initial expedition, which had set out two sum-
mers previously, had carried twelve of the capital's
finest writers across the ocean. The aim, as I understood
it, was to allow these creatives to document and give
an account of the foreign land in whatever style they
saw fit, in order to give the population of the capital a
glimpse of what lay beyond our shores. The land was
evidently rich in resources, for we had negotiated trade
visits twice per year, but none of our leaders appeared
eager to make any further connections or explorations.

Though it was not stated outright, I gathered that the
foreign land was considered quite primitive, and the
artists' reports would serve as a kind of morale-boost-
ing propaganda to the capital's citizens. We were, at
that time, still rebuilding after the Cotton War, and
many great wordsmiths had been forced into menial

work as 'government quills'.

The twelve writers, most of whom I knew personally and some of whom were dear friends, had agreed to remain abroad for six months, though when Calithea arrived to return them home, only Marian Marlowe was there to greet the ship. Reportedly, Marlowe handed the ship's captain a bundle of manuscripts and excused herself with a bow, explaining simply: 'We have rather had a change of heart.'

With our generation's finest wordsmiths in danger of being lost forever, the governor decided it should fall upon me to help bring them back.

I didn't pretend to have forgotten the snub I had experienced from the same man two years earlier, for I too had applied to be a member of the expedition. In the end, I believe I was overlooked because of the reception of my second novel, which was lukewarm at best. The general opinion seemed to be that my writing was too tepid; that I was holding something back and lacked the courage and ambition of some of my peers.

The criticism did not faze or surprise me, for I quietly believed that the critics had in fact got my number. At twenty-eight, I was younger than many of those in the creative circle, and although well-liked in the capital and invited to many of the finest parties, I came to the conclusion that I was seen as something of a wallpaper guest: someone to fill space with polite but unobtrusive color, to act as a leaning post and a kind ear to the more extravagant characters of society. If I was not seen entirely like this, it was nonetheless how I saw myself, and it did not surprise me that this nature might reveal itself also in my art.

It rather appealed to my sense of humor, then, to listen to the governor's request.

'You do not require my abilities as a writer, then,' I said when he told me of his proposition. 'And would rather employ me as a delivery boy.'

The governor met this with his usual badger-like growl. He was a square man of middle age, with a round red face and an animated gray moustache that seemed to work in aggravated tandem with his eyebrows.

'I appeal to you now not for your skill as an artist,' he said gruffly, 'but for your respected character. I am aware that you are a close acquaintance of many of our lost writers, and held in the highest regard by all of them.'

'And you also suspect that whatever wild whim overcame my comrades will not overcome me?' I asked.

He placed his port glass down on the table and reached for the vial beside it. He removed the stopper with care and, tipping his head back, squeezed several drops of the purple liquid into each of his eyes.

'I trust in you to bring them back,' he said, blinking away the discomfort.

I could see the immediate effect of his medicine, his irises gradually transforming from a palish gray to a vivid hazel. It was not a shock to see a dignitary engage in such methods to disguise his age, but it felt rather intrusive seeing the process in person; it was almost like watching an old man undress for his bath, and I felt the need to avert my eyes.

The governor then glanced at his candle clock on the

mantelpiece. The candle had burnt so low that only two markings remained on the wax; we were two hours from midnight.

'Well, Langley, are you going or not?' he barked. 'I haven't all the time in the world, you know.'

In the end I accepted, of course, not least because I had written nothing of value in months and my funds were getting rather low. But something else drew me to the ocean and what lay beyond. I missed my friends dearly, but I also desired to see what had so captured their hearts.

Still, I knew little of where I was headed, and it was with a certain degree of trepidation that I made the three-week crossing from my homeland. I spent the majority of the voyage writing in my cabin, or else stood on deck, gazing out across a gray and tempestuous ocean.

As I looked out at the dark horizon each night from the deck of Calithea, my heart raced as I thought of what awaited me.

I was not surprised to find little fanfare on my arrival. While the crew unloaded the capital's offerings of tobacco and tea, I was met only by Marian Marlowe.

'Langley, you don't know how pleased I am that you're here,' she said, shaking my hand vigorously. 'You've been missed, you know. We wondered how long before they sent someone for us, and we all hoped it would be you.'

Marlowe was a stout woman of middle years, with a strong jaw and a steady gaze.

'Now, how was the voyage? Are you here to stay? You really must, I think. It will change your life. Come, we must celebrate your arrival.'

Marlowe linked her arm tightly with mine and marched me up the road away from the small harbor. She bombarded me with questions about the state of affairs back home, but I was rather distracted by my new surroundings and struggled for words.

I admit that I was at once charmed by my first impressions of the little seaside town. Cobbled lanes wound up the hillside from the rocky shoreline, and the buildings were brown and low, with thatched roofs and hanging plants out front. It did indeed seem less advanced than the capital—I glimpsed paper lanterns where the capital would have had gas streetlights, and several locals who had allowed their irises to gray with age—but the picture was not unappealing.

Halfway up the hill, Marlowe stopped and banged on a yellow door that was wreathed in moss.

'Fawcett,' she bellowed. 'I've a surprise for you.'

It was a few moments before my dearest friend came to the door, but when he did, he pulled it open with his usual gusto and emerged with his great hairy chest exposed in a button-down shirt. He clutched a wineskin in one hand, and his smooth bald head shone in the fading daylight. With a happy growl, he locked his elbow around my neck and embraced me, kissing me all over so that his great walrus moustache tickled almost every part of my face.

'Langley, boy, we've so much to do!' he declared, glancing at the sun. 'Hurry, hurry, we've no time to lose. Get in here, boy, get in, will you.'

He shepherded me inside while Marlowe excused herself, laughing at the reunion of two great friends. Fawcett's abode was cozy—a cottage of oak beams and armchairs and piles and piles of parchments. He rushed me through the living room and out onto a small walled terrace, where a hammock and three chairs looked out over the ocean.

'Langley,' he said, slapping me on the back. 'This is Liana. She's my sun and moon and all the earth, for that matter. Liana, this is Langley, the friend I've told you so much about.'

I removed my hat and shook the woman's hand. She was olive-skinned, with a small, pretty face and child-like hands.

'A pleasure,' I said, bowing.

Liana smiled sweetly and nodded, and it occurred to me then that she spoke none of the capital tongue. To my consternation, Fawcett then barked something in a language that was entirely foreign to me, and she beamed again and replied in a soft, silvery voice that was full of warmth.

Fawcett laughed at the look on my face, which I'm sure must have been quite the picture.

'Fairly easy to pick up, old boy,' he said. 'Give it a few months and you'll be composing sonnets in it. Now take a drink, take a drink, you've much catching up to do.'

Fawcett passed me the wineskin and I took a swig. It was truly the sweetest and most fragrant wine I had ever tasted. Fawcett and Liana also drank from the skin and then Fawcett puffed out his chest and held out a hand to the horizon, as though to present it to me.

'Name a more beautiful sight,' he said. 'You can't, can you? You've landed in heaven, Langley, and it's only a shame it took you so long to get here.'

He reached out for Liana's shoulder and pulled her close to him, kissed her forehead as he had mine, and nuzzled into the nape of her neck. In that moment she gave me a most enchanting glance, like that of a harassed but proud mother, and there was also something inclusive in the look that said to me, 'We both love this man despite all his bluster, and how could we not?' And I felt in that moment an immediate bond with this delightful woman, and an even greater love for the friend I had so missed.

When Fawcett looked up, I noticed for the first time that his face had undergone something of a change. Though he appeared healthy, tanned and well-fed, he had lines on his face that had not been there before—creases in his forehead and around his mouth—and there were even a few white hairs in his great moustache. His eyes, too, had aged. His irises had once been of the deepest mahogany, but their shade was now closer to a watered-down whiskey.

He returned my gaze with his usual sharpness. One of the things I had always admired about Fawcett was his ability to recognize in the flash of a glance what took me long study. Perhaps that was what made him such a keen observer of people and, hence, such a superior writer to me.

'Yes, you see it, don't you?' he said, smiling broadly as

he snatched the wineskin. 'I've aged. We all have.'

I made a noncommittal sound to assuage this comment out of politeness, but it occurred to me that Marlowe too had looked older than when I had last seen her. Her hair and eyes were much grayer than they had been, and her face looked thinner.

'Look at that sunset,' Fawcett said, pointing at the horizon, below which the sun had already disappeared. He grinned as he saw the bemusement that must have been apparent on my face.

'Come, we mustn't lose the evening,' he announced. 'Grab it, yes. Caress it, swallow it whole. But lose it? Never. It would be the most terrible sin.'

He stood and gathered some papers from the table, and Liana rose too and slipped noiselessly inside.

'Won't you tell me what's going on?' I said. 'I've only just sat down.'

I am afraid I failed to hide the trepidation in my voice, for ever since my arrival I felt that I had done nothing but rush around. Although I did not flatter myself that I should be afforded a grand welcome, I had rather looked forward to at least a peaceful evening of tea and supper, in which Fawcett and the others might offer me something of an introduction to this land in which I was a total stranger. I was disconcerted, I had to admit, not only by the new language that perhaps I alone was ignorant of, but also by the strange matter of Fawcett's altered appearance, and an unsettling feeling that I had no grasp of the flow of time.

Fawcett laughed and pulled me through the cottage. 'You've always been such a worrier,' he said, opening the door and leading us onto the street. 'There is noth-ing to worry about here, my friend. You would trust me, wouldn't you?'

He then gave me one of those looks I knew so well. It is a look only certain people are capable of giving; an unblinking gaze that encompasses some absolute certainty that the gazer is entirely in control of his or her destiny, as though they have unlocked some aspect of life's great secret and are desperate to share it with you.

'Of course,' I said, attempting to regain something of my natural smile. 'Sorry, I'm just … the journey was very trying, you know, and I haven't quite got my wits about me yet.'

'Oh, and you'll never get them,' Fawcett announced matter-of-factly. 'That's quite the beauty of it, just you wait and see.'

Liana emerged behind us with a wicker basket of breads, meats, berries, and wineskins.

'Here,' Fawcett said, plucking a purple berry from the bunch. 'I picked these myself from the orchard on the hill. Tell me you've tasted better.'

I let him push the berry into my mouth with his large, rough hands, and it exploded between my teeth with a sour burst of juice. It was indeed divine.

'Onward, friends,' he said. 'Night is at work and dawn hunts her down.'

He and Liana then went off arm in arm down the cobbled lane toward the ocean, and I followed with the sharp tang of the berry still alive in my mouth.

The basement was not unlike those I had seen in the poorer districts of the capital. Barrels were stacked against one wall, low beams made it hazardous to stand up straight, and the room was jam-packed with people.

Fawcett paraded me around, and I met with many of my old friends. They wrung my hand and patted my back and offered me food and drink from their hampers. Hope Cornish was playing a fiddle on a makeshift stage, and a small group was dancing in what little space there was between tables.

Fawcett charged over to Daisy Bradley and Elliot Graham in one corner. They were reading to each other from a pile of parchments and drinking wine straight from the bottle. Fawcett snatched the paper from Bradley's hands, read the first paragraph aloud, and dropped it back onto the table with something like disdain.

'I'm not gripped by it,' he declared, swigging from the same bottle.

Bradley and Graham laughed, and Fawcett passed them his own papers, which Bradley began to read aloud. I watched all this with mild detachment, Liana smiling sweetly at my shoulder, all the while wondering when I might have a chance to catch my breath.

Presently I heard my name being called, and I turned to see Marlowe in the opposite corner, beckoning us over.

'Langley, I must say you complete our picture,' she said. Then she took Liana's hand and kissed it, and exchanged pleasantries in that tongue I had yet to learn. 'Sit, won't you?'

Liana took the spare chair while I sat on an upturned barrel at her side, and Marlowe poured ale from the keg behind her.

'I always feel I can write epics just from the expressions on your face,' she said to me, passing glasses to us. 'You have absolutely no concept of where you are, do you?'

I admitted that I did not, and I was grateful as ever for Marlowe's straightforward manner.

'This town is called Valetti. It's a simple farming town, hardly changed in decades and almost entirely self-sufficient. What little they lack can be obtained from trade with the capital and the other cities overseas. It's a marvel of a place, Langley, as I'm sure you can see already.'

'Of course,' I said. 'And that's all fine, but—'

'The days are short here,' Marlowe said, anticipating me. 'Around eight hours, we estimate.'

I smiled with as much politeness as I could muster, but of course I was rather disconcerted.

'The days are eight hours long?'

'Something like that,' she said. 'There's no way of telling perfectly. The locals here have never used candle clocks and the rest of us see no need to. In some respects, there is nothing different from the capital: the sun rises and follows a predetermined trail across the sky, and then it lands in the sea with a gallant swan dive. But the sun here moves faster, you see. Days come and go like mayflies.'

Marlowe, clearly seeing from my face that I was in no condition to respond, began a conversation with

Liana, who spoke animatedly and with unabashed joy. The two women laughed and drank as they talked, and after I had gathered my wits, I waited for a pertinent moment to intervene.

'But you mean to say that days go by faster?' I said.

'And we age with it, as I'm sure you've observed,' Marlowe said. 'Our bodies are not excused this delightful passage of time.'

'But surely none of this makes sense,' I objected. 'We share the same sun as the capital, do we not?'

Marlowe grinned mischievously, and from that smile I gathered that she had long since stopped trying to fathom the whys and wherefores of her new home.

'But if it's true,' I ploughed on, 'why on earth would you choose to stay? Surely if your lives are shorter here, it would be sensible to return to the place where you might expect to live longer?'

Marlowe drained her glass. 'Drink, Langley, you're behind. Dawn is always hunting.'

Had I not known Marlowe and Fawcett and the others for so many years, I would have escaped from that basement there and then. I felt that I was the subject of some great joke, but at the same time I did not doubt that there was something amiss with the place. There was nothing in my friends' behavior to suggest anything about them had changed apart from their outward appearance, and I felt that I might as well let the night play out as they wished, then set about with the business of the capital the following day.

Quite soon, however, I found myself swept up in the atmosphere of the festival, and I admit that I became quite drunk. I spoke to friends I had not seen in months, and they told me of all their projects, their poems, their short stories and novels; of the local friends they had made, of their lovers, and of afternoons spent in the vineyards, writing beside the ocean, picnicking on the hilltop.

We danced and drank and read in the basement barrelhouse for perhaps two hours (though who could tell?), until Fawcett announced that we were to take to the streets and we went tumbling out onto the cobbles like children dipped in sugar. Locals hung out from their open windows as we paraded up and down the lanes, stopping at certain houses to sing for people who I took to be particularly popular or important, or merely lusted after.

And then, all at once, the crowd dispersed, and dawn broke.

I awoke on Fawcett's terrace, lying in the hammock.

It could not have been long after sunrise, and I felt groggy from the adventure of the previous night. As I let my body slowly come to terms with being awake, I gazed at the little harbor and the line of cafés there with tables outside. The ocean was calm and blue, and I could smell its warm salt on the gentle morning breeze. I listened to the gulls as they squawked from the rocks and swept across my view.

'You're up,' Fawcett said, stepping outside and handing me a cup of steaming coffee. 'I've already written a dozen pages. Here, take a look at them.'

He tossed the papers onto my chest, and I tried to

read them even as he spoke.

'I let you sleep because of your long journey, but that will be the last time. We only sleep for an hour or so here, you know, and some not even that long.'

I looked up from the manic scrawl of his handwriting. 'Fawcett,' I said. 'Why are you here? Just from your eyes I can see how you have aged, and you have only been here for two short years. Why not return?'

Fawcett looked at me in a way he had never looked at me before. It was the way a father might look upon his son before revealing some great human truth that would end the boy's childhood forever.

'We're doing the work of our lives here, Langley, can't you see? And having twice the life we had back home. Have you ever seen any of us so happy?'

I admitted that indeed he seemed happy, as did the others. 'I'm glad you've found Liana, Fawcett. Really, I think she is the most wonderful person. But why not bring her back? You could spend so much more of your lives together. Think of all the extra time you would have to write.'

Fawcett relieved me of my coffee and drained half the mug himself. He smacked his lips and looked out to sea.

'The most wondrous things in the world have the shortest lifespans, dear Langley. And let me counter you with this: if you are able to live this way at home, tell me why you never have? Tell me why none of us ever have?'

I admit that I was unable to offer an answer to this.

'If you saw a golden rose bloom in your garden,' he

said, 'you would water it, love it, treasure it.'

'Well, of course.'

'But if your garden became overrun with golden roses, what would you do?'

I gave a mental shrug. 'I suppose I would become accustomed to them.'

'And cherish them less, yes. That's it, Langley. I would take this life over any other, for it is full of words and love and friendship. It is not soured by the banality of routine, of long, forsaken hours that drag like anchors from your back. Give me a life of lightning bolts, not a vast blanket of gray cloud.'

I took my coffee back and glanced at his papers, reading the words but taking in very little.

'There's a little café on the waterfront. I do my best writing there.' He pointed across the bay. 'Perhaps I shall see you there for an aperitif. Liana is preparing our hamper for tonight, so no need to worry about food.'

He turned to leave, but a sudden thought struck me.

'How might I pay, should I need anything?' I asked.

'You can *write* something, my boy,' Fawcett replied happily. 'These people are creatives, and they value art above all else.'

'But …' I began, but this time I had no counter.

'Listen, Langley. You're a peacock, and the sun is up. Spread those feathers and let the clockwork toys of the capital wind their weary cogs. That's not the life for us. That's not the life for anyone.' He spread his arms before the landscape, as if he were trying to suck the horizon into his chest. 'The garden of life grows evergreen, and many passing through choose not to plant a seed. Plant yours, Langley, and make it golden.'

I kept track of the days in my notebook as best I could, but they came and went so quickly that it was hard to differentiate one from the next. It was as if I were part of some endlessly evolving play, and no sooner had the curtain fallen than it rose again for an entirely new performance.

I spent many of my daytime hours making notes on the town and its people, on the lives being led, thinking that I might complete something of the governor's original assignment. No one was left alone for long, however, for the writers and artists of Valetti valued each other's insights and company, and there were many jaunts into the hills to collect fruits, and trips aboard the fishing dories to read to each other and catch fish for supper.

After a fortnight, I gradually became somewhat accustomed to the faster pace of life. I engaged with Marlowe and others in deep conversations about life and art, how important it was to leave something behind for the ones who would come after. Though the writers lived ferociously, they were not averse to having great debates; in fact, they thrived on them. Their whole lives were devoted to living fully and completely. In Marlowe's words: 'Most people do not find the will to live until they have a knife at their throats. One must do everything in one's power to find that knife as soon as possible.'

The knife was certainly present in Valetti. Of course,

there is more than one reaction to a knife at the throat, and mine was not necessarily a sudden desire to seize the day. I do not mind admitting that when left alone I struggled to focus my mind, so distracted was I by the passage of time. Whenever I saw the sun descend so swiftly into the ocean, it felt like watching my life plummet into some abyss. I was acutely aware that my life was passing me by, and despite the joyous atmosphere of the town and those around me, it was something I could not easily ignore.

When almost six months had passed and I expected Calithea's arrival, I of course considered my position carefully. There was no question of me convincing any of the others to return. I had the notion that none of them would consider leaving until the first of them passed away, and then their impending mortality might put the scare into a few of them and encourage them to put their affairs in order. Until then, I was sure, nothing would entice them to leave their never-ending festival of life.

I admit that I gained no understanding of how the concept of time in Valetti worked. Time, being a human construct, is something so easy to grasp until you re-move it from the context to which you are accustomed, and then it becomes something unfathomable and alien. When six months passed and the ship did not return, it occurred to me that our sun had no connec-tion to the sun I had known all my life. That is, one day in the capital might be the equivalent of three days in Valetti. This meant, according to my calculations, that six months in Valetti equated to only two months in the capital, and I would therefore be required to wait twelve more months until Calithea's arrival.

When I came to this realization, I confess to having experienced a feeling of profound grief. I could not anticipate spending another year in Valetti, despite the many small joys it brought me.

'Do you not value your life?' Fawcett demanded, when I confided in him this feeling.

'Value for life is exactly what concerns me,' I replied. 'Here my life races past, and before long it will be spent.'

'Time is no currency, Langley,' Fawcett said. 'One cannot spend it as one spends copper and silver. Instead it is a gift, something to be treasured. I am surprised at you, I must say. I thought you would take to this place as a duck to water.'

'I have taken to it,' I admitted. 'But it worries me also.'

'Worry,' Fawcett said, and he spoke the word as if it were a poison on his tongue. 'Worry is the least productive human emotion. There is no place for it here, Langley. There is no place for it in humanity at all; it is merely the byproduct of superfluous time.'

Whether I liked it or not, no ship was forthcoming, and so I tried to make the best of a bad lot. A farmer's cottage had become available at the crest of the hill, and I moved in at once. It was old and cramped, but fully furnished, and with the help of various friends we were able to make it comfortable very quickly. It had views of the ocean on one side and rolling hills of livestock on the other, and I found it quite agreeable.

As time passed I was able to focus more on my writing and, though it seemed counter-intuitive, I soon found that I was able to get more done than I would have at home. I also entered into a relationship with a farmhand named Fabia. She was close to my age but seemed in spirit to be much older. She was forthright and direct, would not think twice before saying anything, and had a robust sense of humor that was liable to catch me unawares. She enjoyed painting with watercolors, and she read both my work and the work of my friends with a voracious appetite. She had a rather portly figure and wore her hair in the short style that women in the town favored, and her large dark eyes were a revelation of beauty, capable in one small movement of evoking warmth, vitality, or roguery.

Soon I came to the realization that I was perhaps happier than I had ever been before, and I rarely thought about Calithea's return. When I was reminded of its impending arrival by Fabia, however, a sudden gloom engulfed my heart.

'But you would not leave?' she asked me in her native tongue, for by then I had a perfunctory grasp of the language.

'How could I leave you behind?' I said, though the question was as much to myself as it was a response to her.

At last the day came when Calithea arrived. I had been sharing a bottle of wine with Fawcett and Marlowe outside one of the shoreline cafés while we critiqued Bradley's latest story, when the ship docked and the small harbor soon bustled with activity as crates and baskets were unloaded and loaded. I excused myself from my friends and returned to my cottage to collect the completed work that the writers had deemed ready to be released to the capital. Each of them had completed at least two manuscripts since my arrival, either novels or collections of stories, poems, or essays, and the boxes were so many that I enlisted the help of two farmhands to help me transfer them to the docks.

The ship's captain shook my hand as the work was carried into the cargo hold alongside the fruits, spices, wines, and cured meats.

'No luck, then,' he said, observing that none of the writers had accompanied me.

I admitted that I had indeed failed in my task.

'You have missed quite a time in the capital, I can tell you,' he said. 'I know many people are anxious to hear of your experiences. As for me, I could not imagine a life here. Give me the good old capital any day. Your hold is all ready. You should have everything you need for a comfortable voyage.'

I cannot explain what overcame me in those few moments I spent on the dock. I have thought about it at length since then, and the best explanation I can offer is that worry, that dormant monster, had not only returned in an instant but had spread like a virus through my entire being, and I was suddenly overcome by that horrible fear of death that sometimes visits all of us.

I boarded the ship without saying a single goodbye to any of my friends, old or new. I went straight into my cabin and only came back on deck when we were well out to sea.

Staring at the coastline, I thought of Fawcett and all my friends, of Fabia awaiting my return in the cottage, and what they would say when they found I had departed. I thought of my impending time in the capital; the long, tiresome days surrounded by fools who spent lifetimes brewing medicines that would make them appear younger.

When I realized what I had done, I began to weep openly. I had succumbed to cowardice. I had tried to seize life by running from it. With a deep breath, I vowed never to make the same mistake again.

No one saw me climb the rails. None heard the splash as I crashed into the water.

I began to swim. Toward my friends, toward Fabia, toward the only place I had ever been truly happy. The waves grew as I struggled on; they broke over me, and I was swept along by currents I could not begin to comprehend. I persisted, gasping for breath, desperate to cling to life; breathing, fighting, on and on, until time was lost.

and you realize

Kurt Newton

and you realize you have a big roll of duct tape and you're taping up the seam of a thin plastic wall like a liner that runs underneath the grandstand of a huge stadium

and you realize the seam is failing so you keep taping and you can feel the tape getting sticky in your palm from the friction heat but you keep running the roll down the seam as the wall buckles under your touch

and you realize the seam is coming apart but somehow you manage to keep up and keep it together rolling the tape even faster along the joint amazed that you're keeping the two-inch-wide strip in line with the seam as it runs down and underneath this stadium-like structure unconscious of how you've been moving along with the seam at first perpendicular and now nearly upside down the tape rolling in one continuous strip as if you have the ability to defy gravity like a fly crawling along the ceiling or a water droplet hugging the underside of a glass fixture perhaps trussed in some harness like a construction worker on a special rigging

and you realize the roll of tape is getting lighter in your hand approaching its cardboard core but the seam still has many more feet to go and it needs immediate closure or else the entire structure will collapse and so you watch as the tape winds down doing its job to the very end and you have no other choice as the tape ends and the cardboard falls away like a spent booster rocket but to dig at the skin at your wrist and begin to pull and to your utter amazement your skin begins to part with your arm and dispense its wet fleshy mesh along the seam as substitute for the tape and you feel nothing but relief that the seam is staying put and utter horror that it is your own skin that is keeping it that way and yet you continue to paste yourself like a strip of human wallpaper as the skin peels up your arm and across your chest and down the other arm and back up again across your back and you can feel it tickle as the air moves closer to the nerves and yet you continue to paste and close the seam careful not to push too hard against the surface of the wall as it curves forever downward until finally you run out of seam because you've reached the very bottom of the underside of the structure and your flesh tears free and like a gymnast you flip in mid-air and land on the surface below with a hollow clunk your work boots meeting rusted metal

and you realize you're standing on the surface of an immense metallic body like a submarine or an over-turned ocean liner whose surface is afflicted with a pox of domelike boiler plates riveted into its skin and you begin to walk to try and find your way out of this strange under-the-grandstand-like place before the tape fails and the structure above collapses and it's like walking across an empty battlefield

and you realize as the steam brushes against your raw flesh it burns and the more you try to avoid the drifting clots of mist the more they seem to anticipate your movements

and you realize you have no idea where you are or where you're going or how to get back to where you were before you had the roll of duct tape in your hand and you notice that for every domelike lid there is a dial and a valve and you reach down with your skinless hand and you grip the valve and turn it slowly at first and then more quickly as the needle begins to rise until it reaches the farthest end of the dial and you begin to do this for each domelike lid you encounter running from one to the other as the wispy steam clouds become great white jets shooting out from beneath the rivets and the whole world begins to rumble and the soles of your boots rattle against the metal surface and your body jitters and you begin to shout at the world above at the belly of the great plastic bowl you were assigned to save and you try to scream above the rising din to whomever might still be listening that you have given all that you can give and now it's time to take something back as the first of the boiler-like plates explodes lifting high into the air turning in slow motion until it hits the underworld above and tears a jagged hole in the thin plastic sheath and then another plate launches and then another and another in quick succession and as it rains metal and bits of plastic you simply stand there in awe as the steam surrounds you and your flesh burns away and the weight lifts leaving nothing but your shoes to hold you down and even they begin to melt as the surface of the metal grows too hot to stand upon and as the laces catch fire and the leather sears away you feel yourself begin to rise above the cataclysm floating effortlessly between columns of falling debris pushed aloft by the rising heat

and you realize there is nothing left of your body but a phantom outline like an invisible kite and you float away from all the mess and all the noise and all the world above worlds and under worlds and you drift high up into an empty sky and you look down and see nothing but a smooth blank surface like a skin stretched across the planet

and you realize nothing lasts forever as your bones begin to regenerate and your organs fill the empty hollows and your flesh starts to spread like putty and your skin returns and you feel yourself falling gradually lowering to the surface below and you can only wonder where it is you will eventually touch down

Remnants

Ayd Instone

'It began after I woke from the accident. They said I'd been in a coma for six days. We'd been celebrating at work; we'd just closed a deal that had effectively added another zero to our bottom line. There would be bonuses all round on Monday, but that Monday never came. Well, not for me. On my way home, perhaps driving too exuberantly, too carelessly, I didn't have time to react properly when the car, overtaking on my side of the road, headed straight for me. I swerved off the road to the left. Had I been going at a more appropriate speed, just breaking would have sufficed. My car flew off the road, into the air and over a field twenty or so feet below. I remember desperately turning the steering wheel to the right as if that would get me back onto the road as the ground rushed up to meet me. Strange dreams I can't quite recall. Then stiffness, dryness and pain as I woke in the hospital bed.

'I'd never really feared death. I'd never really thought about it. Why would you when you're young and life's good? I wouldn't say I was an atheist—that would imply some sort of thought on the matter. I never believed nor disbelieved in anything, despite the best efforts of my parents and Sunday school. No, I believed in nothing, except perhaps wealth. Collecting money was what I was good at.

'But I fear death now. You hear me? Now I would do anything, *anything*, to stay alive. It's not possible, I know, but if you had only seen what I've seen. How I long to believe in a god now, your God perhaps, and how I would look forward with jubilation to coming into the sweet arms of Jesus, to meeting Saint Peter at the Pearly Gates of Heaven, or Paradise, Eldorado, Eden. But I know have sinned, and I'd gladly take my rightful place as a denizen of Satan's pleasure if that's what it meant. I'd pass willingly through into the gates of Hades, step into Dante's Inferno and burn for eternity in Lucifer's fire rather than be forced to endure the living hell of the godless death I have now seen.

'How I'd love to agree with you atheists now. With your universe devoid of God and gods. I'd embrace with joy the idea of everlasting oblivion. Oh, to be the flame of a candle with so tenuous a grasp on existence; to be deliciously blown out and extinguished, to be gone, done, and to have escaped the horror.

'You see, I believe I alone understand death—*real* death. You think about a doctor or a scientist, and how they understand the death of the physical body today with our knowledge of anatomy and the brain. They understand it well indeed, far better than the layman. Ordinary people say we die, that the point of death lies at the final breath, the final heartbeat. The scientist knows this is not so. That is why they can pull you back, as I was pulled back. The brain lives on for many minutes after physical death. Do you know what thoughts exist in a mind deprived of blood, of oxygen, of senses, of life? What thinks the man whose body is all but dead? But even that is not the simple case I'm putting here. I'm using that as an analogy for something far worse. I can tell you don't understand. You don't see. Look, when the physical body dies, do not certain organs live on for a while, way on past the end of consciousness? Do the fingernails and hair not still grow? The undertaker can attest to this as fact. Not only that, but the dead, inert body is still riddled with life. Many, many cells live on for some time, that's true, but the bacteria in the body, once symbiotic and essential to life's process, now deprived of oxygen, live on anaerobically and thrive, eating the very body that gave them host. You see it now? You see what I'm saying? Yes, you know that the body, or non-human parts of it we may say, live on and on. They thrive, they live. But what of the mind? The consciousness? The soul? Does that live on?

'The religionists would have us believe in a dualism, that the soul is separate from the body and that one may die but the other goes on. But we are not dual—far from it. We are many, we are gestalt. There are many parts to the body: parts that die, parts that live on, and the horror is that exactly the same is true of the soul.

'That's right. You have a soul, just like you have body. The body is made of many parts and so is the soul, and when you 'die', parts of the body die and parts of the soul die, but something survives. Some part of you goes on and on. I can tell you're not worried yet, and why should you be? You still don't comprehend what I'm saying: some of your awareness goes on, but not all. You, or what you think of as you, will indeed survive bodily death, but in a more random form than you can imagine. A powerless form, a form without form. You will become an itch that can never be scratched, a gloom that can never be illuminated, a despair that can never be uplifted. The human part of you will die, everything you hold dear will die, everything you've ever thought about your uniqueness will die, but you, the thing that you experience, will go on and on, in pain, restless and impotent. You will be an immortal sickness that can never be healed.

'I wasn't sure if it was just a hallucination at first. Certain areas of the room seemed to have a pinkish red hue, others a blue tint. Then, when people approached me, I saw them. Somehow, after the coma, I had a new sense. I could *sense* the things. My visual cortex must have processed this multi-dimensional data into visual phenomena. What did I see? I can only describe them as creatures, but they are more like remnants of that which survives. Remnants of humanity, parts of people's once-human souls, given a form by my brain to make sense of what was there. Just as a dreaming brain gives form to the idle or random processes of chemical re-balance during REM sleep. Just as those images are woven into a visual landscape and narrative that makes sense within the dream, so it is that I can see the creatures. There, draped around the doctor's shoulders was a crab-like hairless monkey. Only its head was an eyeless reptile, like an alligator. Its fleshy tail was wrapped around her neck, squeezing it. One hand was feeling down her top, presumably holding her right beast. It was repulsive beyond compare. I quickly became aware that I alone could see it.

'When I was well enough to walk around the hospital I saw more, far more. There was a man whose chest was covered in green lobsters. They each had a single dead fish's eye for a head, and their claws ended in sharp blades that they were spearing into his heart. A woman nearby had a ten-legged spider clamped onto her head. The creature had a baby's face, and its long tongue thrust deep into her ear, licking and sucking. There were no two similar monstrosities, but they were all invisibly attached to their hosts, sucking, eating, licking, scraping or touching their victims in some vile way. Another man was limping to the bathroom; I could safely assume that he felt some kind of lameness. I gently broached the subject with him, asking if he needed a helping hand, and he rested on my arm as we crossed the ward. He told me he had deep vein thrombosis. I tried not to look at the bruise-coloured scaly sloth, whose claws were embedded deep in his thigh and whose sagging flesh wobbled as the man tried to lift his poor leg. I returned to my own bed and got dressed, knowing I had to get out of this place while I was clear, while I was clean. The young doctor returned and, trying to conceal my horror at the thing on her shoulder, I asked if she was well. She complained of a sore throat, feeling the glands around her neck where the creature had wrapped its disgusting tail so tight. If I could have dared, I would have diagnosed an early form of breast cancer. My guess was that the thing was the cause of her illness, which manifested on our dimension as a disease that science had given a name, but in reality was damage done in real time by the hideous things.

'I thought that once I was clear of the hospital, I'd be clear of the monsters. But no, they were everywhere, clinging onto their human hosts, sucking life to maintain their own putrid post-human existence. I walked down the street. The shops and bars were full of people burdened by the fragments of the disgusting rotting beasts. The people were oblivious to their parasites of course, but not to the pain and suffering they were inflicting. I could diagnose them all now: headaches, cancer, addiction, guilt. All pain, pain, suffering and more pain. All caused or amplified by the things.

'How am I so sure what they are? How do I know they are part human soul? I know. Just as you know when you are not alone, you know when you are in the presence of another sentient person. You know when you are being watched. You know when you are under someone's gaze. Now imagine a feeling of knowing you are in the presence of half a person, a third or an eighth of a person. You'll know all right. By God, I knew.

'As I walked down the street, I heard noises coming from the things. Almost words but not quite. Something attracted my attention. There, lying next to a bin, was a throbbing human heart with a central eye and quivering tentacles. It was mumbling words directed at me.

'I ran out of the town, stumbling, trying not to look or listen. I came to fields and farmland, where there was no one around at last. Perhaps if I could keep away from people, that would work. I climbed a fence into a freshly ploughed field. Then came the worse horror of all. In the trench surrounding, designed to catch run-off from the field to drain it, were what looked like millions and millions of the limbs, bodies and heads of naked baby dolls of various sizes. There were arms with tiny hands, legs and feet, and many beaten-in hairless heads. Some heads were attached to torsos, others were not. Some had closed eyes, some had glazed-over, milky, staring eyes. I stood quite still for a moment, frozen by the bizarre horror of it all, because then it hit me like the stench of sick. These were not toy plastic dolls but parts of real, fleshy unborn fetuses and babies. Unwanted, unloved, unborn and stillborn. I railed to the heavens, where was Jesus? I scrambled out of the field as fast as I could, gashing my leg on some barbed wire, and ran along a grassy path, not stopping until I came to a cliff where the land dropped away down to the shore. I clambered down the bank to the beach. It was sunset, and the sun had already dropped to halfway beyond the western horizon. What was this golden glow that came from the east? As the sun disappeared, this eastern glow became stronger. I waded into the sea, surprised to find it warm, and stared out to the horizon. It seemed like hope. I waded out. I did not feel any sensation of wetness, only peace. I was out of my depth and began to swim.'

'He said all this?' said the consultant as the doctor paused the recording.

'Once we'd got him out of the water and warmed him up,' said the doctor. 'After an hour in the water, he was lucky the hypothermia didn't finish him off. It was so unusual, his ramblings, that I thought it worth recording.'

'He was lucky the sea was calm. Was he really just floating around?'

'A fishing boat raised the alarm. A lifeboat was launched, and they pulled him in.'

'How is he now? Any complications?' asked the consultant.

'We've given a course of antibiotics for the wound on his leg. It looked like it had got infected. The funny thing was how he wouldn't look at it, acting as if he was trying to brush something off that he couldn't bear to look at.'

Both men paused, then the doctor resumed playback.

'Our consciousness, or soul, or whatever you want to call it, is a collective creature just like our bodies. It uses our bodies to feed it, to provide it with energy to remain in its host with some semblance of identity. When that body dies, it falls apart to a lesser or greater degree, and some parts, hanging onto this dimension from some other plane, are trying to continue to suck energy from our corporeal world, just like the once benign bacteria that consume our physical remains. The driving nature of life is to survive, in any state at whatever cost. The true horror I have discovered is that what we call peace, what we call oneness—a clear identity and a form of life that has more meaning than just pure survival—is what we have when we are alive, and that is what dies when we die. And that which persists is not what we would wish to consider, or even call life.'

White as Her Feathers

Jasmine Arch

This time, I found her in a coffee house. Her skin was soft and wrinkled, her hair as white as the feathers she wore when we first met.

She didn't recognise me, of course. That was the way it always went.

I'd lost track of the number of lives I'd lived, searching for her over and over again. Some may think it's a blessing not to lose your memories while you rest between one life and the next. But they've never experienced it.

Every life you live, everything you are, leaves its mark.

When I lived the life of a dog, I learned to trust unconditionally and to appreciate simple joy.

When I lived the slow, trickling life of an oak, I learned patience and the art of letting time drift by. Fallen leaves floating away on a stream.

It was during my days as a swan that I learned to love. Swans only choose one mate in their lifetime. When I met her, I knew: I'd be waking up next to her every day of my life.

Her feathers were a delicate, translucent white. The graceful curve of her neck mesmerised me. The mischievous glint in her eye sparked a pleasure I'd never felt before.

Then she fell to the bow of a hunter. And the part of the swan that stayed with me when I finally laid that body to rest was the part that missed her.

So I spend my days searching. Some lives I find her. My joy in those lives is endless.

Once, I was a hound and she my master. Centuries later, the roles reversed. In another cycle, I saw her eyes in the face of a father of four.

Every time, I had to woo her again. Let her get to know me. She doesn't share this accursed memory.

After a life spent searching in vain, there she was. Sitting alone in a coffee shop with a book in her lap. I wiped my suddenly clammy hands on my skirt and glanced at the white feather tattooed on the inside of my wrist.

She looked up at me. Her smile widened as I carried my espresso over to her table.

'Is this seat taken?'

John Doyle Remains

Stephen Oram

I had a girlfriend who ate my scabs. She pulled them off my tender skin, turned them around in her fingers to observe their particular contours, and then popped them on the end of her tongue. She said she enjoyed their scratchiness. Then, with a twinkle in her eye, she'd snap her tongue into her mouth and swallow. I was young, head-over-heels in love, and enthralled by the romance of her ingesting me, albeit a fragment that I was about to shed. Once swallowed, she'd begin kissing me on the pink skin revealed by her action, but that's another story and not one I'm prepared to share with you. Throughout my long life the intensity of that intimacy has been integral to who I have become. I nourished her, as she devoured and later defecated my crust. The memory has clung to me like the object of her attention.

'What? Stop staring at me. I can see you're processing this; your eyes are green. I know you're taking it all in to extract what you want and discard the rest, just like her. Arching your MeCat back like that each time you deposit a snippet for the record is cute but unnecessary. You can stop that now.'

These days, she takes a scrap from old social media footage, from when we were together, and reposts it as if that's the whole story. The trouble is, only I know it's a sliver of the reality and such a tiny sliver that it no longer contains any truth. She's still taking parts of me and turning them into something for herself, but the romance has gone—from both sides. I get the feeling she wants to possess me, desperate to be embedded in the story of my life. She wants to feature in the legacy I'm leaving with you when I die in a few days' time, and I'm not sure that's what I want. If it is, then I'll choose, not her.

'What? You're still staring. It is my choice, you know. It's my choice who owns me when I'm dead, and no I haven't decided yet. And yes, I will give you instructions before I fall off the edge. I know I've tried many times. This is the last. How can I be sure? Because I've used all but one of your lives. I've rebooted you eight times. This is your last.'

I need the right person to act as me once I'm gone, to keep me alive and relevant. A custodian who can continue to comment on the commentary and correct the errors where it's misguided. Someone to carry on, to develop my persona beyond the one I leave behind and persist with my presence in the world to come.

And, to be honest with you, a mad scramble among the beneficiaries of my will for that privilege will be so unseemly. Not the way I wish to begin my Legacy Life. I know, they're my children and grandchildren. They're not here, are they. They're not exactly weeping at my bedside. If only their mother was. If only we had stayed together. Mind you, she was allowed to fade away gracefully, not famous enough to warrant an entry in the wiki of the deceased, and certainly not significant enough to society to continue to contribute, to live on virtually directed by a custodian. Maybe if we'd been a couple when she died she'd have got one, although I reckon she was better off simply choosing a static selection to be remembered by. Free from the burden of appointing a custodian to manage the dynamic post-death entry in the way I have to.

'Yes, yes, there are a lot of well-meaning posts popping up wishing me well. Yes, I know they are sincere, but would you give ownership to someone who barely knows you? Oh, you have. To me. Fair enough, but you had no choice and I do. And although it's painful to say, once you've set me up on the wiki and passed your curation on to whoever I choose, you'll be reset to factory settings and become the property of someone else. You don't have to worry about getting a version of you perfected, knowing it's the starting point from which your future self will grow and be judged.

'You're not using this conversation as part of my legacy, are you? If you are, then scrub it. Immediately. Goodness, what if I was to die suddenly and these were my last recorded thoughts?

'Look, it's ready for harvesting. I've been waiting for this for days. Things take so long to heal at my age. What do you think? I reckon that at the end of this life it seems perfectly reasonable to take possession of that particular memory and turn it into a new one for the next.

'Make sure you capture this.

'Well, that came away easily, didn't it? Look, I'll pop it on the end of my tongue. Gulp, and it's gone.'

Self-romance, that's what my life has become. Lonely, isolated and famous. Destined to live on in some people's memories and to be born as new memories for others. Thank goodness for Legacy Life. Where would I be without it.

'Yes, I know—the task in hand.'

Who was in charge of that monstrous birthday montage they sent me last year? Was that Fred? Is he really a child of mine? Did you see the mess he made of it? Wrong people, wrong emphasis, wrong everything. And as for his prim and proper offspring and that stuck-up wife. Well, we can strike him off the list of potentials, I'm not having him as the owner of my future. And I certainly don't want him in charge of choosing the next successor; in a couple of generations I'd be nothing more than a celebrity pastiche. No, he's definitely out. Mattie. She's always been the closest to me. Growing up, she 'got' my art. She knew how to involve herself with it in a way nobody else ever has. I wish Mattie wasn't married to that awful woman and didn't have those loathsome kids. I have to think beyond the immediate to who she will bequeath the responsibility, and she has not proved at all capable in her choice of companion or in the creation of her children.

I could abandon this whole escapade and refuse to be entered into the wiki and not begin a Legacy Life. I could die and fade, only remembered by whatever art remains. It's an attractive proposition. The trouble is I suspect that a bunch of wannabe friends and casual lovers would come out of the woodwork and put together their own version of me from the pieces they've misappropriated over the years. There's plenty of footage out there for them to make of me what they will. And they would. Of that, I'm sure.

So, we come back to the central question. When the archive is ready for a custodian, who shall that be? A professional maybe? A fan of my art maybe? A lottery winner maybe? Now a lottery sounds fun, almost like a piece of art in itself. I wonder. Could I insist on a core of my entry that nobody can ever change, and then let loose with the rest? Now, that would be a thing. A lottery for a five-year contract to be my custodian. Paid for by my estate. That way I'm owned by everybody and nobody. In fact, I would own me in a way that's never going to be possible with a single definitive custodian. I like this a lot. They won't—the offspring and their offspring—which makes me like it especially. It's exquisite.

'MeCat? Yes, you. Your eyes are red. Are you refusing? Will you stand in my way because—because of what? It's never been done? That's a good reason to do it. It's not in the spirit of the wiki or the contract for Legacy Life? I disagree, it's about conveying the essence of me, the artist. You don't understand? You don't need to understand, you need to do. As you're told. That's the difference between us—I don't. You do. I'm alive. You're not. I'm creative. You're a machine. Legacy Life and the wiki of the deceased are for me and my kind. Neither are for you and your kind. I can ride roughshod over your protocols. I insist you do this.'

I take ownership of this. I am the one who owns me and will always be the one who owns me. No matter what morsels are taken from my life to fortify and boost other egos.

'Amber eyes, that's better. You're getting it. Green again. Thank you. You've made an old man at the beginning of his next life very happy.'

Sky High with Janine

Vaughan Stanger

Marcus Farrell stood at the edge of the Sky-High Pool, wobbling slightly as he dared himself to overcome his fear of heights.

'Good to see you here, Marky. You took your time!'

He flinched. No one called him *that* to his face. He turned around and waggled a forefinger to indicate his annoyance. This moment would be noted in his ledger of slights.

The goateed, Speedos-wearing middle-aged man reclining on one of the roof-top loungers shrugged his dismissal of the implied threat. No name sprung immediately to Marcus's mind, but most of Alpha tower's residents would be familiar with his from the *Financial Times* or *Bloomberg Live*. Only the ultra-wealthy could afford the apartments in this tower, with its keycode-accessed poolside. While not himself a resident, Marcus's status as one of the financiers of the development had secured him the privilege of visitor access—a privilege he'd put off exploiting for the best part of a year, until now when his between-projects ennui finally got to him. Even so, he wondered whether he'd made a mistake.

Don't look down!

Marcus gulped hard and closed his eyes. When he opened them again, he'd already turned his head to his right. The city's skyscrapers trembled in the heat haze but soothed him with a reminder of the fortune he'd made there. He didn't bother to look to his left, towards the squalid blocks and low-rise conglomerations where the no-hopers lived. They did not concern him.

Sneering laughter came from behind him. 'Go on then!'

He was about to snap a retort when a gentler voice said, 'Take no notice. Most people wobble a bit the first time.'

Marcus glanced to his left. A smiley man of indeterminate age, wearing a psychedelic t-shirt and no-brand shorts, squatted on his heels a couple of metres away. Well-muscled arms sported tattoos Marcus struggled to make out against his skin tone. Pool attendant, maybe?

'I'll be fine,' he said.

Marcus turned his back on the water, took a deep breath and grasped both handrails of the metal ladder tightly enough to whiten his knuckles as he began his descent. His anxiety notched higher with every step. When he reached the bottom one, he gritted his teeth and forced himself to let go. The tips of his toes barely scraped the bottom. As if being out of his depth here wasn't bad enough, his knowledge that the Sky-High Pool deepened towards its middle only compounded his anxiety. He made a mental note to send a sarcastic email to the architect.

'About bloody time!'

He ignored the heckler and struck out towards the Beta tower. Not once did he turn his gaze sideways, never mind down. Happily, a surface-swimmer like him could see almost nothing of what lay beneath the pool. Which was definitely a good thing, especially on his first visit. For now, he remained content to execute his slow, poorly synchronised breaststroke, while trying to ignore the sour, nauseous sensation building in his head.

Halfway across the fifty-metre span and panting hard, Marcus grabbed a handrail and wiped the water from his stinging eyes. With hindsight, he should have trained for this swim and also brought his goggles. He didn't doubt he could complete the length but felt anxious about making it back without taking a protracted break first. Lingering at the Beta poolside while catching his breath would look odd given the absence of loungers and other facilities there, due to the ongoing dispute between Alpha's ultra-wealthy residents and Beta's mundanely prosperous types. As he would surely endure further ridicule from Goatee Guy, he decided it would be best to get it over with sooner rather than later.

As he turned himself around, someone's hand collided with his right temple with enough force to push his head beneath the surface.

'Get out of my …!'

The gurgling underwater soundscape distorted the front-crawler's scolding.

Semi-dazed by the blow, and with water already entering his mouth and nose, Marcus found himself wondering which way was up. Before he could solve the puzzle, powerful hands grabbed his shoulders and pulled him back to the surface.

'Stop struggling!'

A woman's voice: stern, commanding.

He spat out sour-tasting water. 'I'm okay—'

'Just *relax.*'

Still dizzy from the blow, he complied, albeit reluctantly, and allowed her to tow him back to Alpha's poolside. The rhythmic pulsing of her leg-kick underneath him proved surprisingly soothing, plus it gave him the perfect opportunity to flip the bird at his assailant, who had just messed up a kick-turn at the Beta end, but the slow handclaps accompanying his return to Alpha punctured his feeling of moral superiority.

After filing a mental note to identify Goatee Guy and ensure some financial flak hit him where it hurt, he clambered up the metal steps and sat on the edge of the pool, trembling as he gazed at his rescuer. Lithe, long-haired, and slick as a seal, with her black one-piece contrasting strikingly with her pearly skin, she had commenced what seemed likely to be a length along the *bottom* of the Sky-High Pool.

He turned to the pool attendant.

'Who is she?'

The man shrugged. 'Calls herself Janine.'

Something in the attendant's tone suggested he didn't believe her name was genuine.

'What is she, a lifeguard?'

'Apparently.' Delivered with a wink.

Marcus nodded to acknowledge the joke—which was fair enough in the circumstances—and held out a hand.

'Marcus Farrell,' he said.

The pool attendant shook his hand. 'Reef, at your service.' Then he stood up and bustled off to do whatever needed attending to.

Marcus turned back to the pool, expecting to see Janine swimming back towards him. But other than the bully-boy swimmer, who was now approaching the Alpha poolside, the Sky-High Pool was empty.

Two months passed before Marcus felt ready to return to the Sky-High Pool. Regular sessions in his Essex mansion's gym and indoor pool, plus an assortment of quasi-legal performance enhancers, had transformed flab into muscle, breathlessness into endurance.

Several residents sprawled on the loungers, bathing their expensive tans in smog-filtered sunlight. Goatee Guy was absent, as expected. A mutual acquaintance had identified him, while an enticing but dodgy cryptocurrency opportunity had delivered a financial coup-de-gras.

Janine was also absent. Still, he wouldn't need her again, thanks to his training regime.

'Good to see you here again, Mr Farrell.'

The pool attendant smiled at him.

'Thanks ... Reef.'

He was mildly impressed to have remembered the man's name. Perhaps there was hope for him after all.

After adjusting his goggles, he jumped in with his legs tucked—making a big splash, as was typical of him. No easing himself in this time! He pulled hard, kicked strongly, every action in synch.

As he neared the midway point, he submerged his head. A sleek black-and-white shape passed underneath him. The chiaroscuro queen of the Sky-High Pool trailed her fingers along the transparent bottom, as though to remind him of the distance to the ground. He shuddered at the thought but didn't let his unease turn into panic. After letting a speedy front-crawler pass, he resumed his breaststroke.

When he reached the Beta end, he clung to the ladder and turned around, eager to catch another glimpse of Janine.

Ah, there she was: treading water a metre of so from the Alpha ladder while chatting to Reef. When the conversation finished, she grabbed the lip of the pool and executed a flawless backstroke start, followed by a surface dive. A remarkably short time later, her head bobbed up a body-length from Marcus. Her auburn hair trailed behind her like seaweed. It was the first time he'd obtained a good look at her. As with Reef, she had one of those weird young–old faces, as if she'd been around the block a few times but hid it well, if not quite perfectly—a feature he invariably found attractive.

'I'm Janine,' she said.

'Yes, I know. Reef told me.' Janine's knowing nod

coupled with an appraising stare sucked some of his usual confidence from him. Still, nothing ventured …
'And I'm—'

The slightest of splashes announced Janine's departure. In any case, she probably knew his name already via Reef. But it was rude of her to depart so abruptly— and he didn't let anyone get away with *that*. He kicked hard against the end wall but struggled to keep pace with her while she glided along the bottom. As his head lifted out of the water, he looked towards the Alpha end. Reef was standing next to the ladder and making a diving motion with his hands. His implication was clear. If Marcus wanted to meet Janine properly, he would have to do so on her terms. The prospect made his guts squirm like a nest of vipers. He trod water for several seconds while waiting for his equilibrium to return.

That was better. Now he felt calm enough. Now he was ready for Janine.

After sucking in the deepest breath his lungs would hold, he thrust his arms and head downwards and slid underwater. With his feet kicking hard and his goggles tightening around his eyes, he could finally see the world beneath the Sky-High Pool's floor.

Two hundred metres beneath him, people bustled around the plaza, on their way to work, or the shops, or wherever: the have-nots grinding out ordinary lives while lacking any kind of escape route. For once, Marcus experienced no sense of vertigo as he gazed at the world below. Instead, his vantagepoint induced an exhilarating feeling of superiority.

That was the moment he noticed Janine. She was gazing at him from the other side of the pool's floor.

His heart hammered in his chest as Janine raised her right hand, acknowledging his presence. Then she arched her back and dived. She plummeted into the chasm between the towers, a human arrow destined for a bloody, broken end. He closed his eyes. On reopening them, he saw no sign of a body. The pedestrians bustled as before. Janine had disappeared before hitting the ground. Which was impossible.

Then again, everything about Janine was impossible.

All too aware of the pressure in his lungs, Marcus kicked for the surface. Emerging in a burst of spray, he gasped for breath for several seconds. Only when his chest stopped heaving did he commence a slow swim back to the Alpha poolside. After hauling himself part-way up the metal steps, he sat trembling on the pool's edge. Once he'd recovered his composure, he got to his feet and peered downwards past the left side of the pool's structure, followed by the right. Having observed nothing unusual on the ground, he turned to Reef.

'How the hell does Janine do that?'

Reef's forehead crinkled. 'Do what?'

'Didn't you see?'

'I saw her swimming underwater, if that's what you mean.'

It wasn't what he meant, but he couldn't see any advantage to pressing the point. He turned back to the pool. As he'd half-expected from look on Reef's face, he immediately spotted Janine swimming underwater, dolphin-kicking towards the Beta end with her usual aplomb.

'So, do you want to meet her?'

Marcus turned back to Reef. 'Um, how do you mean?'

'Oh, come on, man! I can tell you're into her.'

Long habit prompted Marcus to shrug, but he suspected Reef would see past it. He wondered what the catch was, or indeed whether he was Janine's catch. Not that it mattered. If a problem ensued, his legal team would deal with it.

'Okay,' he said in tones suggestive of no more than a passing interest. 'What's the deal?'

Reef grinned at him. 'You'll need the after-hours code.'

Marcus pointed towards a sign next to the access door. 'So, the pool area doesn't close at 10 p.m.?'

Reef gave a conspiratorial wink. 'Not to Janine, it doesn't.'

'Okay.'

'If you just let me have your number, I'll …'

Marcus shook his head. 'No, just show me on your phone. I've got a good memory.'

Reef grinned like a man who had expected his gambit to fail.

'It works after 1 a.m. Okay?'

Marcus nodded. 'Sure. I'll be there.'

He knew he couldn't resist the invitation. From time to time, he liked to embrace whatever weirdness was on offer, provided no harm came to his reputation. Happily, he already possessed everything he needed to guarantee his security.

As he squeaked across the concrete in his designer flipflops towards the changing cubicles, he chuckled to himself.

Of course he'd be there.

After deactivating the security camera above the access door using an app on his phone, Marcus tapped the numbers into the keypad. A single beep signalled success. The door to the roof clicked open, admitting him into the night-time warmth, two hundred metres above the glow of streetlamps and the intermittent growl of lorries. After confirming that the poolside was deserted, he located and deactivated the three security cameras monitoring the area.

Satisfied no one could snoop on him, he strode across the warm concrete towards the lapping water. Lit faintly from below, the Sky-High Pool tantalised him with its possibilities. Assuming of course that Janine was present. Perhaps that was the catch. If so, it was a feeble one. He would enjoy a solo swim and depart with a shrug.

After placing his towel and phone on a lounger, he undressed to his swimming shorts, then descended the ladder until only his head remained above water. Shivering even though the pool retained some of the warmth from the day, he tugged his goggles into position and commenced a vigorous breaststroke. Janine or no Janine, he revelled in the illicit thrill of swimming in the between-towers darkness.

Halfway to Beta, he turned over and floated on his back, his hands sculling gently. As he half-expected, a pair of hands grabbed his ankles. He gulped air deep into his lungs and allowed himself to be pulled beneath the surface, like a sailing ship snared by a monstrous squid. Strong arms encircled his ribcage; calves clamped his shins. Janine dragged him deeper, unseen but irresistible, until his shoulder blades touched the floor. But how was that possible? A moment ago, she had been underneath him.

Marcus rolled over so he could look downwards. There she was, waving to him from a distance that logic declared impossible while—equally impossibly—floating between the towers. Driven by an urge he didn't understand but could not resist, he pushed his arms downwards, kicked hard, determined to join Janine in her magical realm beneath the Sky-High Pool. He followed her heedless of danger. She responded by diving even deeper.

The pressure in his lungs grew inexorably. Bubbles of air began trickling from his lips. His thoughts became ever more detached as the darkness hypnotised him with its promise of the comforts of drowning.

Without warning, a pair of hands clasped Marcus's wrists and jerked him upwards. He willed himself to rise faster, towards the feeble glow above him. One more tug, one last kick of his feet. His lungs now empty, water surged into his mouth. So close, but not quite close enough …

Marcus woke with a gasp, his body spasming like a newly landed fish on a boat deck. He blinked repeatedly, struggling to focus. His mind was muzzy, like someone had drugged him. The anticipated thrills with Janine had turned sour indeed.

Finally, his vision cleared enough for him to take in his surroundings. From his position in the middle of the scuffed vinyl floor, he observed the room was unfurnished. Dusty, crumpled venetian blinds covered French doors leading, he assumed, to a balcony. This wasn't the apartment of any of Alpha's residents, and probably not of anyone who lived in Beta, either. While undoubtedly have-nots when it came to accessing the Sky-High Pool, they were well off by most people's standards.

'Where am I?'

He addressed the question to himself, but as he rolled his head to the left, he noticed a middle-aged woman with straggly, greying hair sitting cross-legged in the corner nearest the half-open door to the hall. Dressed in no-brand denims and white blouse, she would not stand out in any crowd. She nodded, as if satisfied by his re-awakening.

'Think of it as Omega,' she said.

Marcus knew the Greek alphabet well enough to understand the implication, but as if to emphasise it, the woman walked over to the window, pulled the cord to raise the blinds, and opened the doors. Marcus got to his feet, a little shakily, and joined her on the balcony, which gave him an excellent though giddy-making view of the Alpha and Beta towers from about half a kilometre away. This flat, which he suspected didn't belong to his captor, was situated a few storeys below the level of the Sky-High Pool. Even so, he held the railing tightly.

'How did I get here?'

The woman chuckled. 'I had help, of course. Also, the codes to Beta.'

A suspicion bubbled into his mind. No, it wasn't possible. How could she be Janine? As he stared at her, the crows-feet at the corners of her eyes dissolved, to be replaced by the flawless skin of a *Vogue* model. Her hair straightened and darkened. A fringe hid her forehead.

'Oh!'

All too possible, apparently.

'Which is the real you?'

Janine shrugged. 'Whichever suits me.'

'Okay …' He paused to gather his thoughts. 'So, what are you: a witch, an illusionist or my kidnapper?'

'Whichever suits *you*.'

That was him told, he thought, although not greatly enlightened.

He considered making a dash for the door, but Janine tapped her phone and raised it to her face. All things considered he would do better to learn about her plans first.

Janine asked, 'Is everything ready?'

A male voice responded, loudly enough for Marcus to identify its owner.

'Yes, all locked and loaded.'

'And all clear below?'

'Yes, the plazas are empty,' Reef said. 'Looks like all the residents got the message.'

Sirens wailed in the distance. Flashing blue lights approached on the three-lane carriageway. The emergency services had got the message, too.

'Janine, what's going on?'

No answer.

He turned around. The room was empty. Janine had departed without him noticing.

So: an illusionist at the very least.

He ran into the hallway and tugged the door handle. Finding the door locked, he returned to the living room. A pile of his clothes awaited him. Janine had hidden them, too, along with his phone, which sat on top, buzzing. He snatched it up and read her message.

I used to be a nasty piece of work. Not an ultra-wealthy one like you, but able to indulge my whims. I used my talent to lure loners into swimming pools at night. I seduced them with promises I had no intention of keeping. Left them with mutilated little fingers. Sicko, huh? Still, your idea of fun is also perverse. Sorry, but your app doesn't work the way you think it does. (But I digress!) Anyway, I got careless (like you!). I picked a victim who had his own special talent: the ability to plant a compulsion in someone's mind. Reef (not his real name, of course) lured me. Afterwards, he offered me a deal: use my talent to help other people or repent at my leisure behind bars. Guess which I chose! But ten years on and our activism hasn't produced many tangible results. If we're ever to bring this shit to an end, we'll need a lot of money. Yes, I do appreciate the irony. Which is why you're here, Marky. Reform now or repent at your leisure.

> *It's up to you. Not convinced yet? Okay, just remember what Nietzsche said about gazing into an abyss. Now, if you take a look at your clock app, you'll see the timer is running. You should have enough time to get back to the balcony.*

He tapped the app.

10 …

9 …

8 …

He stepped outside.

3 …

2 …

1 …

Puffs of smoke burst from both ends of the Sky-High Pool, followed two heartbeats later by the sharp crack made by explosives. Marcus looked on open-mouthed as the middle of the structure sagged. A moment later, both ends detached from both pool-sides. The whole edifice crashed to the ground amid torrents of water. Even at this range, the cacophony reminded Marcus of every car crash he'd ever viewed in his home cinema. As the roof-edge waterfalls subsided, shards of glass, brick and metal continued to fall onto the deserted space between the towers.

Marcus released his breath in spurts. So *that* was what Janine and Reef had been up to. Yet nothing they'd perpetrated had required his presence. Why then was he here?

Before he could figure it out, shouts—no, that was cheering!—erupted from the balconies around him, then a moment later from a neighbouring tower block. Within seconds, waves of jubilation came from tower blocks and low-rise developments further away. Marcus stepped back into the living room as if propelled by an irresistible force.

This was Janine's abyss, he realised. It was the daily experience of the people who lived in this neighbourhood, the poor, the old, the infected, the illegal: everyone who was separated from him and his peers by an unbridgeable gulf of wealth and privilege.

And now the abyss was gazing into him.

Gazing hard.

His phone buzzed again.

Now check your photos.

He did.

Janine had been telling the truth. The app had been recording his activities, not making them secure.

Boots pounded in the hallway outside the flat as he read her third message.

Reef has told the police where to find you. They'll find enough evidence to charge you, but I expect your lawyers will get you off, unless we use those photos and videos. We reckon each is worth one million pounds to the right people. That's a hundred good causes we could fund with your wealth. So, if you don't want anyone else to see them, let us know and we'll give you a list of bank accounts you

> *can donate to. Not fair, you say? Well, look at it like*
> *this: the recipients will definitely put your money*
> *to better use than you have.*

The door shook under the force of gloved fists.

'I'm locked in!'

And locked up good and tight by Reef and Janine if he didn't cooperate with them.

Even if the photos and videos remained under wraps, the media would have a field day. Merely to be charged with involvement, however tenuous, in the Sky-High Pool's destruction would be bad enough. His reputation in the Square Mile would never recover. There was no way back from that.

'Stand well back!'

After a resounding crash, the doorframe splintered, followed by the door slamming against the wall. Four policemen wearing visored helmets and body armour surged into the hallway. One of them pointed a taser towards him.

'On the floor! NOW!'

Marcus complied. The officer read him his rights while a constable tightened cuffs around his wrists.

As the police marched him across the plaza, cheering erupted. Marcus looked up at the people waving from balconies. Presumably, they believed he'd destroyed the Sky-High Pool. In a way, he had.

But as Janine had hinted while shattering his illusions, there was so much more he could do.

Making money was *his* talent. It was time he put it to work.

Frosting

William F. Aicher

Sofia licked the frosting from her fingertips. Two minutes in the past, the cupcake had existed in her hands, borne of a strange conflagration of flour and sugar and God knows what else.

Eggs. Probably eggs. And butter. Sticky, creamy butter.

Animals in the yard. The farm fields. Stinking and eating and existing for no reason other than for mankind to eat them or their young or their milk. Milk created for *their* young. Babies in our stomachs. Mothers and fathers on our grills.

But the cupcake and the egg. The egg inside the cupcake and the baby inside the egg. Not yet a baby but just the chance of life. Maybe something else. Possibility and virtue combined into one. Honest and devoid of vitality. Nothing but potential.

Cracked and broken. Mixed and beaten and stirred. Baked in an oven. Into something tasty, utilitarian, and disposable. To be expelled from our bodies—the bad parts. The good, absorbed. Until we die. Until Sofia dies. Not from the cupcake. But from life. That subtle killer we all fall victim to somewhere along the journey.

The sugar rushed through her body. A drug of everyday life. The most addictive, some say. But she savored it.

Bathed in it.

Reveled in it.

For that one instant. Until it was gone. Metabolized and spent.

More. She wanted more. She had to have more. But as she reached for another, her hand discovered only vacancy, and she tumbled headfirst into the hollow emptiness of the cupcake pan. Darkness surrounding her as the world turned from day to night. A microscopic existence, where mantises are great towering mammoths and amoeba circle like a swarm of goldfish in the sky.

Where do you go when you stop believing in the story? In the part where you had a role to play? After you've suckled your fingertips like those baby cows and their mothers' teats, eager to consume before the farmer came and stole your lifeblood for himself?

The same place everyone else goes when they step out of the dark and begin to transform into those they become. Who, in retrospect, is who they always have been and never will be.

Sofia found herself there. In the nothing of time.

Waiting for the clock to tick again and for her body to grow large so she could devour another cupcake.

But they were gone, the cupcakes. And she was here. And there.

Somewhere nowhere everywhere.

Wherever the sun shines and the day breaks and the sky falls on a winter's eve. Sparkling like diamonds in the snow, blinding eyes and warming hearts.

Peppermint and icicles. Like frozen fire in a Christmas hearth.

A crumb on the table. Speckled in strawberry icing.

Plucked like a flower. Into Sofia's mouth.

As she consumed the world.

The Daughter of Echoing Hills

Soumya Sundar Mukherjee

As I walked, I saw the passers-by giving me a strange look.

Most of these people looked sad, some horrified, some a little disgusted. One of them made eye contact with me for a second and promptly looked at the other way, murmuring something, perhaps the name of God. A woman was coming from the other side of the road with a little child toddling by her side; she saw me and at once picked up the child to her breast and moved away so that the child may not see me.

I found it a bit amusing, but my mind was busy thinking about the face in the photo.

The sun was behind the Echoing Hills on the west, the last reddish hue rested upon the rocky shoulders of the hill. The streets of the town were full of fashionably clothed men and women and children, although, unlike big cities, the road was almost free from an endless rush of cars. From a music shop I could hear an old melodious Bollywood number being played. I stood for a moment to listen to the song that told of unrequited love.

The streetlights came up. My legs were tired. It was expected, because I had come to this town from under the rocky feet of the Echoing Hills.

I heaved a sigh. The upward journey to this place had been exhausting, but my mind told me that only here could I find the woman in the photo.

This part of the hilly town was full of fast-food stalls; the delicious smell of fried eggs came from one of them. But I didn't feel hungry. I went to the old man who was reading the evening newspaper under the streetlight.

'Excuse me, Sir. Have you chanced to see this woman somewhere?' I asked, holding out the photo.

The man looked into my face and smiled sadly. 'Oh, it's you.'

'Do you know me?' I asked, a little surprised because I knew fully well that I'd never met him before.

'I think I should say, "I don't." But I can tell you where you can find this woman,' the old man said, putting the newspaper down.

'You know where she lives?' I could hear the excitement in my own voice.

'Yes. You need to go up, my boy.'

'Up?'

'We call her "the daughter of the hills". She lives at the top of the southern portion of the Echoing Hills. You'll see her hut from half a mile's distance,' he said.

The daughter of the hills? Strange nickname!

'Thanks a lot.' I was, however, delighted to have the information I needed. I couldn't wait to see her.

'There is one more thing I want to tell you,' he said.

I looked at him. He shook his head sorrowfully and said, 'I pray you may find your peace, my boy.'

He walked away, tucking the newspaper under his arms. I didn't realise what he meant by that, but I was happy to get the direction to the house of the woman in this photo.

Her face haunted me like a restless spirit. My legs still hurt, but I prepared myself for the mount.

The road to the southern part of the Hills was somewhat steep, and I needed to sweat a lot to reach there.

But I was not afraid of it. I wanted to see her.

I wanted to see her; I wanted to kiss her; I wanted to …

That unknown voice whispered again in my mind, 'Do you love her?'

God knew that I wanted to say, 'Yes.'

'Echo is always imperfect,' she said.

The hut was situated just a few metres away from the profound cliff, which stood towering over a rocky plain. I had glimpsed at the bottom from here and felt a little dizzy.

The inside of her hut was not very spacious; at one corner stood a rope-cot, and by its side was a pitcher of water. Some books rested on a small table. The whole place smelt of wet soil and the night jasmines in a china vase. I looked through the window. The grand silhouette of the Echoing Hills could be seen from here in the bluish evening. A couple of stars were already up the hill. The full moon looked like a deep yellow dish upon the eastern horizon, preparing to come up over our heads.

'If you don't mind,' I said, 'I'm not particularly a fan of echoes. Can you tell me where I've seen you before?'

Her eyes were dreamy, and a little smile hung on her lips. Spellbound, I stared at that heavenly face. But it didn't seem that she had heard what I just said.

'Echoes are weird things. Sometimes they throw at us the same fragments of words again and again. These hills often echo; tell something to them and they'll give you back the same answer, the same broken piece all the time.'

I took out the photo from my pocket and observed her face again. *Yes, she is undoubtedly the one.*

She saw what I was doing and said, 'You think you saw me somewhere. Don't you think that's an echo, too?'

'Maybe,' I said. 'But where exactly does this echo come from?'

'All echo comes from the hills.' She stood up and picked up a book from the table. 'Look at this.'

I took it from her hand and found that it was not a proper book at all: only the hard cardboard covers, front and back, remained of it. The real book was missing.

'Once I was angry and throwing things. I threw this one from the cliff, although I knew well that it was forbidden to throw things from the cliff. The whole book, mind you, with near three hundred pages was hurled into the depth of the hills. The next day I discovered *this* on my table. Only the covers, not the whole thing.'

I said nothing and examined the book, or what was left of it. She said, 'The Echoing Hills send back echoes of everything you throw to them. But echoes are imperfect, as you can see.'

So, the girl I think I love is a bit eccentric about echoes. Not a problem for me.

I showed her the photo again. 'I found this in my pocket this morning, and I have no idea how it came to be there. But when I saw it, I felt that I needed to see you.'

She glanced at the photo and said, 'Then?'

'I came to the town, trying to find you. I should not keep it from you that a lot of the townsfolk were looking strangely at me, although I don't know why. An old man, who seemed to have known me but denied it, gave me the direction to this place and said that I'd find you here. Now tell me, don't you find all this a little mysterious?'

She kept quiet for a moment, looking at the big moon over the hills. Then, with a sigh, she said, 'There are mysteries which are best kept hidden from some people.'

'Why?'

'Because they give nothing but pain, echoing pain.'

The moon was up above the hills; its colour had changed into a soft hoary. The top of the hills looked like someone had poured liquid silver upon them.

'Why did you want to see me?' she suddenly asked.

I, almost like a machine, answered, 'Because I think I love you.'

She laughed and it sounded so sweet in this lonely place full of moonlight over the shadowy hills. I felt that she took pity on me, but I was happy with that. *I wanted to hug her, I wanted to kiss her, I wanted to …*

I felt an irresistible attraction to this woman I barely knew. And I thought she knew it, too.

'You sound quite like him,' she observed.

'Him?' I felt a pinch of jealousy inside my heart.

'A boy named Ranjan,' she said. 'He, too, said he loved me. He said that he could give his life for me. He said that a smile on my lips was all he wanted.'

'Then?'

'Then it turned out that he wanted more.'

She seemed to be lost in a dream as her eyes fixed upon the distant peaks under the moon. After a long silence, she said, 'I want to tell you about Ranjan.'

'I don't want to hear about him.'

'You have to. This is the story of the echo, this is the story of these hills, this is the story of the photograph in your pocket.'

She knows how to persuade me.

'Tell me about Ranjan, then.'

'Ranjan loved to play with the echo,' she said dreamily. 'He used to stand by the cliff and shout things to the hills. The hills always echoed the last part of what he said. I often forbade him to do so. These hills are holy; they see us, they watch over us, they guard us. And we must be reverent to them. I often told him that one shouldn't be playful with the Echoing Hills. But did he ever listen to me?'

'Did he?'

'Never. He often came to me and said how much he loved me and how he wanted to see me smile. With this kind of talk, you know, you can win a lonely woman's heart. He was about to win my heart.'

'Then?'

'Then I came to know that it was not my heart he wanted.'

She wiped the corner of her eyes and said again, 'He wanted a thing far less valuable than my heart.'

As soon as she said this, I noticed how perfect a body she possessed. She was tall and the curves of her body were amazing. I felt the beast inside me roaring, wanting to pounce upon her and discover the nakedness under her clothes, madly chanting, 'I want you! I want you!' But I managed to keep myself calm. The story was interesting.

'What happened then?'

'One day he stood beside the cliff and I sat in front of my hut. The full moon was there upon the hills. He shouted to the hill, 'I want you!' and the hill replied, 'Want you! Want you!'

'He turned to me, and I could see the unnatural hunger burning in his eyes. I knew what he wanted.

'He said, "I want you".

'I protested, but he was so strong! He hit me on my face and tried to kiss me. I could see the drool hanging from his teeth under the moon, just like a rabid dog. His face came down, and I could hear he was whispering, "I can't wait more. I want you! I love you."

'That was the moment I realised he didn't love me at all. It was not love, but lust, a ferocious lust. I saw in his eyes that there was little love for me, only a burning lust. I could take it no more.'

Suddenly she stopped and looked at me. I said, 'What happened then?'

'The hills became angry.'

The way she uttered the words suddenly gave goose-bumps all over my body. I looked at the quiet hills flooding with white moonlight and felt an enormous presence watching us constantly.

The hills don't need words to …

'What happened to Ranjan?' I asked.

'He never got what he wanted. I prayed to the hills, and they gave me strength to save myself, but don't ask me anything more.' Her voice suddenly became concerned. 'I beg you, please go away from here. Never come back and you might find peace someday.'

I remembered the old man. *Why do people assume that I need peace?*

'I don't need peace,' I said. 'I need you. I love you.'

She smiled. 'Now you're starting to sound just like him. Almost like an echo.'

'What's it with you and the echoes?' I knew that I sounded a bit rude, but I was curious.

'The echoes are answers the hills give back to you,' she said. 'When nobody's around, the hills speak to me.'

She saw the disbelief in my eyes and said, 'Come outside.'

We walked out of the hut and stood near the cliff. The distant town behind us was dotted with thousands of tiny lights upon a mass of darkness. And the hills in front of us, in front of the cliff, stood like a giant with several moonlit heads. I turned my gaze; she was looking so eerily beautiful that my breath almost stopped.

Was that a silver twinkle in her eyes?

'Ask the hills something,' she said, unaware of how stunning she looked. 'The answer must be yes or no.'

Still I couldn't take my eyes off her. Her hair was fine strings of silver, swaying a little in the gentle breeze that blew from the direction of the town, and the moonlight glistened upon her skin like a pearl in water. I stared shamelessly at the shadow under her breasts.

'Ask the hills a question,' she said. 'If you want to know about your love.'

That was a great idea. I walked to the cliff and faced the dark hills who waited in a profound stillness. My voice trembled when I spoke.

'Does she love me? Say yes or no,' I shouted to the dark hills.

'Now wait a couple of seconds,' she whispered.

We waited. My voice was lost in the unfathomable darkness beneath.

Then the echo answered in a thundering voice, 'No.'

I looked back at her. She smiled the sad smile again.

'Don't you really?' I asked, surprised, as if I was certain that she would love me.

'The hills never lie,' she said.

I felt something shatter inside my heart. *No, no, it can't be!*

I said, 'That's simply stupid, you know. The echo only gives back the last portion of the sentence, doesn't it? I can always rephrase my question.'

'You think the hills don't understand what humans think?' she said. 'Very well. Ask again.'

Standing by the edge of the cliff, again I shouted, 'Does she love me? No or yes?'

A couple of seconds' waiting. There was no answer.

I waited for a 'yes'. But nothing came. No echo.

I looked at her. She only shrugged.

I asked it again. The dark hills swallowed my voice once more and gave back no answer.

Okay, one last try.

I shouted my question for a third time to the dumb hills and they preferred to remain silent again. I felt as if they were watching me in my futile attempts to have an answer to a question they didn't like; they were watching me like unknowable dark gods looking down at some insignificant fly.

I faced her. 'The hills don't dare to answer me, but you can do it. Tell me, do you love me? Yes, or no?'

This time the whole area reverberated with the thunderous voice of the hills answering my three questions at once, 'No! No! No!'

It was as if the hills were forbidding me to take the next step.

'Please go!' she pleaded. 'The hills have answered. You shouldn't be staying here anymore.'

The sound died down and the whole place sank again into a deep silence. The gentle breeze suddenly stopped blowing, and it seemed that the hills were holding breath to see what would happen next.

I saw tears rolling down her cheeks like little white gems in the shimmering moonlight. Her body looked like an angel from heaven, and I wanted her.

A fiery desire flared inside me, and I felt that this sensation was vaguely familiar, as if I had experienced it earlier somewhere, like an echo returning, or déjà vu.

I wanted to have her in my arms, beneath my body. I wanted her.

I wanted to hug her, I wanted to kiss her, I wanted to …

I attacked her like a carnivorous beast, and she fell onto the ground. 'Get away!' she shrieked. 'I don't love you!'

'I don't care about your love!' I growled. 'I want your body. Now!'

'That's why you'll never get it. That's why the echo will never give a "yes" to you.'

Her kick hit me in the groin, and I found myself almost flying towards the cliff.

I'm falling!

I never imagined that her slender body could muster such strength. For a moment, the fear of death engulfed me. I blindly reached for something to hold on, and luckily found a creeper to hang from. I clang to it as my body dangled like a spider over the edge of the cliff.

She came to the edge and looked down at me. When she spoke, her voice wasn't angry, but I found a strange sympathy in there that I didn't understand.

'Tell me one thing before you go down, you poor soul. Tell me, do you remember anything in your life before this evening, before going to the town to get directions to my place here over the hill?'

I suddenly froze. *I don't!*

'You still don't remember me, do you, Ranjan? Even

after seeing the photo you always carried in your pocket?'

Oh my God!

'You come to me every evening, Ranjan, after that incident. After we both got cursed by the Echoing Hills. You're just an echo, my dear: a hollow body without any past, any future. Just like a book cover without the real book, or a fragment of a whole sentence; just an echo. You're a shadow without a past, only filled with a blind passion to catch me, to have my body. I pity you, Ranjan, and I'm sorry for you.'

'You're lying!' I screamed. 'Who told you I remember nothing?'

The hills echoed, 'Nothing! Nothing!'

She said, 'Touch the back of your head.'

Still dangling, I did so and at once realised why the townspeople were repulsed at the sight of me. My hands tried to touch the back of my head but couldn't; the fingers only went deeper.

I don't have any back portion of the skull!

'An imperfect echo of the boy I once threw down from the cliff,' she said. 'Since then, every evening this echo comes back to haunt me. This is *my* punishment, too, Ranjan. The hills remind the daughter that she made a mistake by throwing a man from the cliff. I'm reminded of my crime, just like you. Everything you experience is nothing but an echo, including the man who told you the way to my hut.'

'No! No!' I screamed, now remembering everything. 'How many more times do I have to …?' I realised that my hand was losing grip on the creeper.

'Every echo finally dies at some point,' she said. 'That's hope enough for us. Goodnight, Ranjan.'

I saw her turn away slowly from the cliff. I couldn't see her anymore, only hear her voice, 'See you again tomorrow.'

Again. Tomorrow. Tomorrow.

Her words echoed inside my vacant skull, and I let go of the creeper I was clutching.

The dark hills watched quietly as I fell. The uneven, rocky ground seemed to be speeding upwards to embrace my body, and my empty skull prepared for the impact.

It wasn't totally hopeless, I thought.

Perhaps tomorrow, or in tomorrow's tomorrow, or in a faraway tomorrow, I'll stop echoing my today.

tragic, silent, ravenous souled

Nadia Steven Rysing

It is the hundred and eighth day.

That means something. That number is supposed to mean something.

But I can't remember what.

It should mean something to have spent a hundred and eight days climbing this mountain, alone but for an owl and the ghost of Jack Kerouac.

It has not been as lonely as it could have been. Jack's not a bad sort. Him stopping every few minutes to cough up enough blood to flood your boots … well, it gets old pretty fast. Sympathy can only last until you see chunks of his liver sprayed out over the ground ahead of you. It is one thing to be with a dying man. It is another thing to have to trek through his insides with bare feet.

The liver always grows back by the morning. He's

good company when he first wakes up, until the cirrhosis kicks in again and the rage of liver failure slams into him like a freight car. His eyes are so yellow now they glow, almost like they can light up the path ahead of us. Lamplights. Floodlights. Golden rays against the cold, whipping snow.

The owl, on the other hand, is an asshole. Never said anything to confirm that, but you can tell when those big eyes stare you down and make it clear which one of you is a predator and which one of you is roadkill.

I was never a mountain climber. Never intended to be one, anyways. Yet here we are, Jack and I, summiting the face of Mount Shasta in nothing but our own skins. We walk forward again and again but each dawn we find ourselves at the same base camp.

I tried to stay awake for twenty-four hours to see what force knocked us back down. When I hit twenty-three fifty-nine, the owl swooped in and tore my eyes out. I passed out from the pain and ended up back in my bedroll next to Jack.

The eyes grew back.

They grew back the next three times I tried.

Every time I've heard the word 'samsara' I've tossed it aside as litter on the trail.

Once I asked Jack why we were there of all places.

He argued, 'You said you wanted to see mountains again.'

I replied, 'I was quoting Tolkien. If I had to end up with a Catholic writer with a tendency to ramble, I would have picked him over you.'

Jack laughed. 'Why would he be here? Tolkien never

had to go to hell.'

Once I was told of a hell where women who died in childbirth would be forced to drink their own menstrual blood. Thank whatever gods there are that I never had children.

I questioned, 'Is that where we are then? Hell?'

'Where else could we be?'

'Why would hell be a mountain?'

Jack commented, 'I climbed a mountain once, looking for God. All I found was myself. Desperate, hateful, arrogant little me.'

Then he leaned forward and I rubbed his back, glancing away as he spewed out blood. When there was nothing left in him, he stumbled forward, the owl flying ahead.

The owl never stops flying. I've never seen it even flap its wings. It just sails. Day or night, it sails.

Five nights ago, I thought I saw a dove. I pointed it out to Jack.

Jack asked, 'Does it have an olive branch?'

I shook my head. 'It has nothing.'

Jack replied snottily, 'Then stop wasting my time.'

This morning, I started bleeding. First from my gums and then from my throat. By the afternoon, I could feel pieces of myself in my mouth.

'Is this how it starts, Jack?' I asked. 'Dying?'

Jack argued, 'You have to be dead already to be in hell, Sam.'

I disagreed, 'I don't think that's true. I don't think that's true at all.'

Jack vomited out the smaller lobe of his liver into the

snow. He fell to his knees in the retching and I knelt beside him, holding back his growing hair like we were two girls at a college bar who had just a little too much to drink and were just a little too much in love with each other to let the other be sick in peace.

I don't love Jack. I don't think I could love him unless he loved me first.

I was in love a thousand times before the mountain. I loved every boy I had ever met and some I even fell in love with twice. There was one I thought I loved but his heart was stuffed with sawdust and the gold in his eyes was nothing more than rust.

I didn't know who he really was until he died.

I thought if I was to wander hell, I would find him here with me.

The owl calls out, and we see the rocks ahead have begun to shift. The shackles are ready for us. We have travelled too far today. We must be held back until morning, until we can return to base camp once more. To go forward is for the mountain to collapse. To head back is for the mountain to collapse. To remain with freed hands … you understand. There is no other choice.

Jack has been too weak to lock himself in his manacles. I have helped him before trapping myself, before exposing my living form to the elements.

For the past eight days, the owl ate Jack's liver while we were strapped to the mountain. It hasn't touched mine yet. I think it is not decayed enough yet to warrant interest. Maybe in another hundred and eight days and nights I will be rotten enough to tempt it too. Or maybe it is as it was in my own life—my suffering was never from my own pain but the pain of other people. Experience could not make me flinch, while witnessing would send me into catatonic shock.

On this night, the night I first vomited the pieces of my liver, I turn to the dying form of Jack Kerouac, as green and yellow as a string of beans. Even through the fierce snow, I can count every one of his ribs.

Jack murmurs, 'All dark nights of the soul must be black and starless. We cannot find the light if there is no dark.'

I plead, 'But why does it have to hurt?'

In words softer than I had ever heard or will hear again, Jack says, 'So you know that you are still alive.'

On the Bus

Robert Guffey

Dramatis Personae

I jerked awake when the bus sped over a pothole. I held my hand in front of my face and squinted through the glaring sunlight pouring in through the windows. Outside lay an endless stretch of desert filled with cacti and tumbleweeds and reptiles. The last time I was in the desert, when I was twelve years old, I got bit by a rattlesnake hiding beneath the sand. Linda, my step-mother, had to suck the venom out of my leg and spit it out onto the burning desert clay. That was when I first realized how much pain lurked just beneath the surface of the world.

The intense light of high noon, the cloudless sky, the arid wind, the sweat-stained t-shirt sticking to my back: all of this reminded me of the day I almost died. I wondered, *Where's Linda right now?* I hadn't seen her in years. I was angry with her but couldn't quite remember why. There was so much I couldn't remember, so much of my life I had misplaced (my car keys, my soul, same thing). Sometimes I wished I could wander into a used bookstore and stumble across a book titled *101 Things to Do Before You Kick Off*. Anything to give some direction to my 'life', if one could even call it that.

My brain was cloaked with fog. I hadn't been getting much rest. To fall asleep on a moving bus wasn't the easiest thing in the world, particularly when you've suffered from insomnia for as long as I have. Since the incessant migraines began. Since my mother died.

I shifted in my seat. Somehow I had gotten myself twisted into a fetal position. Thankfully, for the past twelve hours or so I had had a seat to myself; this meant I could stretch my legs out at last. Only four new passengers had boarded the bus at the last two stops. The area we were driving through was perhaps the most desolate I'd ever seen. The desert was disturbing to me, particularly at night when the air itself seemed laced with ghosts.

My dreams had taken strange turns since entering the desert. For three nights I'd had recurring dreams of Elizabeth lying motionless on a white carpet, her face drenched in blood, her open eyes black as night and staring right through me into another world (perhaps this one). Just before the bus lurched over the pothole, I had been attempting to kill a kitten over and over again, but it refused to die. It just kept rubbing up against my leg, purring, purring. No matter how much I tortured and crippled the animal, it refused to stop loving me. When I awoke, the sweat staining my body was as much from fear as it was from the heat.

I stood up to stretch, glancing at the other passengers as I did so, at least those few I could discern amidst the glare. An old woman clutched at a clear plastic oxygen mask with one arm while her other arm attempted to strip the mask from her wizened, frightened face. A teenager rapped silently to nonexistent music as his mouth bled a purplish, syrupy substance onto the floor. An old man sat hooked to an IV unit filled not with blood, but with a dark mass of squirming insects. A young raven-haired beauty in a skimpy red belly-shirt lay in the middle of the aisle pleasuring herself while a circle of twelve-year-old boys gathered around and watched with rapt attention; she was naked below the waist, where her crimson-lacquered fingernails probed and caressed the serrated, spider-like pincers that protruded from her hairless vagina; the clicking of the pincers as well as her moans were drowned out by the perpetual, metronomic cough of the engine. A silver-haired, middle-aged man in a business suit—oblivious to the chaos around him—reached into a patent leather briefcase and pulled out the severed head of a reindeer. He kissed it, hugged it tightly while tears moistened his haggard cheeks. A muscular blond teenager, tanned copper by the sun, removed his NO FEAR t-shirt and carved the words THE BODY IS OBSOLETE into his chest with his own fingernails. A husband and wife screamed at each other at the exact center of the bus; the man grabbed his wife's hair and yelled, 'More noise please!' then began beating her head into the emergency exit window while the woman laughed and laughed and laughed. A dwarf in a green tuxedo vomited on his feet; if only his feet were attached to his body, the situation would have been less disgusting. A nude man, death camp skinny, eyes as distant as Antarctic ice, sat curled up on the sticky floor, shivering, shivering, peeling skin off his left shoulder, revealing the black starry emptiness just beneath the surface of his pale flesh. A man with the head of an eagle, wearing a red silken robe, lay sprawled on his seat reading a thick book titled *The Last Four Seconds of Your Life*. He only had a few pages left. The very back of the bus could not be seen clearly; feasting in darkness, nameless gibbering things with ropy tentacles sucked on the bone marrow of lost hitchhikers, naïve waifs who'd ended up on the wrong road at the wrong time. Judging from the sounds that emanated from those distant shadows, I was glad every nook and cranny of the bus was not visible to me.

Yes, all the passengers were still there, just as they had been for the past … oh God, how long had it been? Five days? Five years? Five *decades*? Who could say? I only knew that it felt like an interminably long time.

Dramatis Personae (Cont.)

[Memo to driver: as much as possible, please discourage soliloquies from supporting members of the cast. Thank you.]

171

Near the front of the bus sat two of the most inscrutable characters I had so far encountered on this cross-country trip. One I referred to as 'the Man in the Iron Mask,' the other as 'the Pink Gorilla.'

The Man in the Iron Mask was almost seven feet tall and had very bad posture. Perhaps this was a result of his having to bend over in order to enter doorways or avoid being hit by low-hanging tree branches, or even just to hear what people were saying. He was thin, dangerously so, and seemed to live on liquid protein which he drank through a bendy straw that he slipped through the jagged slats of his black metallic mask. The mask was oversized and looked rather uncomfortable. Just keeping his head up must have been a constant balancing act. He was dressed all in black: black turtleneck, black Levis, black combat boots with the laces flapping loose. I could only imagine the dark clothes made the heat even worse. Perhaps he enjoyed pain, or felt it was his duty to suffer like a monk in a hairshirt. The mask was foreboding and reminded me of something one might have found in the dungeons of the Spanish Inquisition. I was dying to ask him why he was wearing the thing, but I couldn't think of a way to bring it up that wouldn't be awkward or embarrassing.

The strangeness of the Man in the Iron Mask paled in comparison to the Pink Gorilla, who sat on the opposite side of the aisle. The Pink Gorilla was, in fact, a pink gorilla. The seat seemed to quiver slightly beneath the strain of his considerable girth, and his bowed muscular legs threatened to puncture a pair of knee-shaped holes in the back of the two seats in front of him. He sat hunched over, taking up the breadth of two entire seats, while reading what looked like a tiny red hard-cover book. He seemed engrossed in the book. I was dying to know the title, but—again—couldn't think of a proper way to ask. I disliked it when people spoke to me on the bus, and assumed others felt the same way.

I wondered where the Gorilla was going. Was he flee-ing the ruins of a failed love affair like myself, heading west for fame and fortune, or just looking for a brief vacation from reality in the badlands at the edge of the world? Of course, these questions could be asked of any of the passengers, but for some reason none of them fascinated me as much as these two characters.

On a whim, I decided to push aside my reticence and approach the odd pair. They didn't seem to know each other. During the entire ride, I hadn't seen either of them even *glance* at one another. Weren't they as curious about each other as I was of them?

[Memo to driver: please make certain our hero moves up to center stage slowly, apprehensively. There's no reason to hurry this; we have plenty of time. Never sacrifice aesthetics for expediency. Thank you.]

I strolled up the aisle and purposely dropped some change on the floor. A nickel and two dimes landed on the Gorilla's foot.

'Sorry,' I mumbled.

'That's quite all right,' the Gorilla said. 'Allow me to help you retrieve your specie.' Gingerly, he closed his book and set it aside on the armrest, then leaned down and tried to pluck the coins off the floor. This was difficult, as his fingers were large and clumsy. The coins did nothing but slip between his fingertips. 'Uh, sorry about this, old chap. I guess I'm not quite as, uh … helpful as I'd like to be.'

I suddenly realized that the Gorilla sounded a lot like a character in an old radio show that my grandfather used to play for me as a kid. The show was called *I Love a Mystery* and featured the adventures of three freelance troubleshooters named Jack, Doc, and Reggie. Reggie, played by a young Tony Randall, was a stereotypical anal-retentive Englishman, the kind who says things like 'Blimey!' and 'Pip-pip!' a lot and probably exists only in the American imagination.

'It's okay,' I said to the Gorilla, 'I can take care of it. Kinda my fault, anyway.'

I was able to collect most of the coins with one sweep of my hand. In my peripheral vision I could see the Gorilla growing uncomfortable, pushing his tiny pince-nez glasses up onto the bridge of his flat nose just to have something to do with his hands. From this new perspective my view of the Gorilla had changed. Before, I had seen him as calm and stoic; now I could see that he was a bundle of nervous energy. Without a book in his hand, he didn't know what to do.

'Say, uh, what's that you're reading?' I asked.

At first he acted like he didn't know what I was talking about. 'Mm? What do you—? Oh! You mean this little thing? Nothing, nothing at all. Just a … guidebook. Yes, that's exactly what it is. A guidebook.'

I laughed. 'From over there it looked like Mao's Little

Red Book.' The Gorilla just stared at me with a quizzical expression. 'You know, back in the '60s? All the protest kids were wavin' around a little red book, looked just like that, by Mao Tse Tung?'

The Gorilla sniffed, as if offended. 'I wasn't alive back in the '60s.'

I was taken aback. 'Well, neither was I. How old do you think I am?'

He studied my face intently while stroking his furry chin. 'Mm ... forty?'

'Forty?' I burst out laughing as the reason for his mistake dawned on me. The Gorilla seemed hurt; perhaps he thought I was laughing at *him*. This was one sensitive simian. 'I just realized that we all probably look alike to you. I'm twenty-eight.'

A chagrined smile appeared on the Gorilla's face. 'I-I'm not used to all this, I'm afraid.' His brown eyes darted from side to side, perhaps looking for an escape route, like a claustrophobe on a stalled elevator. 'Social interaction, I mean. I spent most of my childhood in London attending school. My parents were very strict, and I had to spend my whole childhood studying. This is my first sojourn outside England. I'm sorry if I offended you.'

I waved my hand. 'Don't worry about it. Uh, where in London did you go to school?'

'The Royal Institute of International Affairs. You've probably never heard of it.'

Over my shoulder a metallic, sepulchre-sounding voice boomed throughout the tiny bus: '*Piss* on the Royal Institute of International Affairs! It's nothin' more than a breeding ground for jumped up bureaucrats with too much power. Did you know it was formed in 1920 by the same Anglo–American Elite who met at the Versailles Peace Conference in 1919? They've orchestrated every single major international conflict since the end of World War I.' ('Oh, dear,' the Gorilla muttered beneath his breath, 'another conspiracy theorist.') 'People like that, if you can even call 'em people, have no national boundaries whatsoever. They control the media, the military, the medical community, you name it. The Institute is just a minor cell of a world-wide secret society infested with sadistic magicians aligned with the Bilderbergers, the Council on Foreign Relations, the Freemasons, the Knights of Malta, etcetera etcetera. I'm sure you get the picture. I've been researching this shit since I was fourteen. I find it very suspicious that a graduate of such a nefarious Institute should end up in the seat across from me on a crowded cross-country tour bus.'

The man who had delivered the preceding soliloquy, the Man in the Iron Mask, glared at us through the jagged slits that covered his eyeholes. He had moved to the edge of the seat and was now leaning forward expectantly, waiting for an answer. I could see his hand inching toward the inside pocket of his black jacket, as if prepared to pull out a weapon in the event that the answer was not to his satisfaction.

The Pink Gorilla seemed unperturbed. 'I did not, dear Sir, claim to be a *graduate* of the Royal Institute of International Affairs. I simply stated that I had *gone* there, the past tense being the operative component of the sentence.'

'Okay, so how come you left?' said the Iron Mask. He'd slipped his hand inside his jacket and was now toying with something within. A knife, perhaps? A gun?

'For a variety of reasons,' said the Gorilla, 'one of which is that I simply didn't want to stay.'

'Ah, I see, a wiseguy.' The Iron Mask chuckled. 'Imagine. All this time I've been sitting right next to a comedian and I didn't even know it. How about telling us *why* you didn't want to stay.'

'Hey, maybe you should lay off,' I said. 'What business is it of yours?' Gun or no gun, the man's abrasive attitude was getting on my nerves.

The Gorilla placed a calming hand on my shoulder. 'Though I have no particular reason to share such information with this gentleman, I find it's much less inconvenient to humor the purveyors of autocratic imprudence than to become embroiled in a senseless altercation.'

'What the fuck does that mean?' the Iron Mask said. 'Call up my old lady! She'll tell you I ain't never been imprudent in my whole life!'

The Gorilla continued with his train of thought as if the man had said nothing: 'In a sentence ... I was not at all pleased with the cavalier attitudes my peers displayed toward the severe methods our instructors insisted on employing in their obsessive attempt to depopulate the planet. Is that a satisfactory answer, or shall I elaborate?'

'I knew it!' The Iron Mask slammed his gloved fist into the palm of his bare hand. 'I *knew* those assholes

created AIDS to depopulate the planet. I've been following the paper trail on that story for years, a-and to
have it confirmed *now* in the middle of fuckin' nowhere?
Incredible! It defies all odds.'

'You're jumping to conclusions,' the Gorilla said. He
spoke so softly it was almost as if he was whispering. 'I
said nothing about—'

I felt it coming a second before it hit. The migraine
struck me in the center of my head with the force of
a spear. I screamed and toppled over onto the floor.
Everything went black.

[Memo to driver: please do your best to make certain
the lights shut off with disarming abruptness here.
The audience should be wondering if something has
gone wrong in the theatre. Thank you.]

I came to with my face pressed into pink fur. I was
vaguely aware of the Gorilla cradling me like a baby.
I couldn't quite see him, though. Everything was still
blurry. 'Elizabeth?' I mumbled. 'Elizabeth?' I wasn't
quite sure where the hell I was.

'Here, sniff this, kid.' The Iron Mask's tomb-like voice
drifted into my consciousness from somewhere far,
far above me. I felt a plastic straw slipped gently into
my left nostril; my right nostril came next. It was like
returning to the crib: mother offering up her breast out
of pure instinct, no strings attached. I sniffed heavily.
As it trickled down the back of my throat, the sweet
syrupy substance tasted a lot like ambrosial wine.

My whole body snapped to attention; my eyes transformed into wide white discs and my spine felt like a live wire whipping about inside my body, every nerve ending charged with electricity.

The Iron Mask chuckled. 'That stuff'll bring you to every time. Got quite a kick on it, doesn't it?'

I couldn't stop moving my right foot. 'Wow, I-I feel pretty good. This is the best I've felt in … in *years!*'

The Gorilla cast a hard glance at the Iron Mask. 'What did you give him?'

'Oh, nothin' special, guvnor.' He briefly mocked the Gorilla's accent. 'Just my unique Protein Shake concoction.' Though I could not see his eyes, I felt as if he was winking at the Gorilla.

'My migraine's totally gone. For the first time in years my migraine's *totally* gone!' I laughed. 'I feel like running a mile in a minute flat.' I leaped off the Gorilla's lap and began pacing up and down the aisle.

'Feels like that the first time,' the Iron Mask said, easing the straw between the slats covering his mouth. 'You get used to it.' He slurped down a few gulps of the shake as well.

'Please calm down,' the Gorilla said, 'you might upset … the driver.' He lowered his voice upon uttering those last two words.

A sense of foreboding descended upon me; I wasn't sure why. It had never occurred to me to *look* at the driver, much less upset him. Slowly, slowly, I glanced over my shoulder …

[Memo to driver: please make certain spotlight is placed directly on rear curtain. We had some problems with that last evening. Thank you.]

I had never noticed it before: a red curtain separating us from the front of the bus. I saw malformed shadows floating behind the thin material. No, I didn't want to look at those shadows. I didn't even want to *think* about them. I didn't want—

'Say, why don't you go on up and say hello to the driver,' said the Iron Mask. There was a hint of sarcasm in his voice. 'I'm sure he's a very nice fellow.'

Absolute fear gripped my gut.

'Don't listen to him,' the Gorilla said. 'Focus on something else, on the here and now.'

The Iron Mask just chuckled and shook his head. 'Tell us how long you've suffered from these migraines, kid.'

A few seats down somebody yelled out: 'Hey, can't you be quiet up there?'

The Iron Mask stood up, all six feet eleven inches of him, and shouted back (imagine the Voice of Imminent Death booming at you from down a long, dark tunnel): 'Shut the fuck up or I'm gonna go down there and shove your head up your asshole sideways!' The Iron Mask's comment received no response. He sat back down and said, 'Go on.'

I said, 'Uh, what was I …? Oh, migraines. I've been suffering from them for about sixteen years, I guess. Since I was at least twelve. I think I'm responsible for half the aspirin consumption in the United States.' (*That strange curtain* … why did it seem so familiar?)

'You might want to try an herbal supplement called Feverfew instead,' the Gorilla suggested. 'It's better than pharmaceutical products because it has no side effects and—'

The Iron Mask waved his hand in the air. 'Fuck that shit. Just stick to my shake, kid. It'll get you where you need to go.'

The Gorilla sighed. 'Interesting that you should advocate a transient method of treating pain that seems more aligned with the allopathic field supported by the very same Institute you reviled earlier, rather than the homeopathic field which operates *outside* the restrictive parameters of the military–pharmaceutical establishment whose cryptoeconomic interests are shored up by illegal drug sales around the globe—a practice of which you apparently approve.'

After a brief pause the Iron Mask said, 'What the *fuck* did you say?'

'My point is obvious. The amphetamines of which you are so enamored are utilized by the very elite you fear in order to instill a slavish robotism amidst its poor and middle-class work force, thus supporting the capitalistic tenets you rail against in your daily life.'

'What the fuck, how the hell do *you* know what I "rail against" in my daily life?'

The Gorilla sniffed and turned his head toward the window. Through a slight smile he said, 'Oh, I've dealt with your kind before. You're very good at reeling off a litany of facts concerning the conspiratorial nature of history, but when it comes down to actually doing something to change the situation you're like a spoiled little brat playing rebel; you want to bite the breast that feeds you while still suckling from a poisoned teat made appetizing to you by the very same media manipulation about which you claim to be so knowledgeable.'

The Iron Mask reached into his jacket and pulled out a .22 revolver. 'You just fucked up big time. Nobody questions my sincerity and gets away with it.'

The Gorilla didn't even flinch. Instead, he began cleaning his glasses with a white handkerchief. 'Your species never fails to puzzle me. Those of you most sensitive to the encroaching fascism now threatening your freedom seem most *eager* to commit violence against people with whom you disagree. Very ironic, what?'

'You're not a fuckin' person! You're a fuckin'—'

I leaped in front of the Iron Mask's gun. 'Hey, hey, cool it, man! He didn't do anything to you.' It was difficult to keep my full attention on the Iron Mask, what with that strange curtain pulling at my gaze …

'You needn't protect me,' the Gorilla said, calmly opening his little red book and resuming his reading. 'I'm not afraid to die. Unlike some people, I don't get my courage through a straw.'

I knew what was about to happen. I grabbed the Iron Mask's wrist—too late. His muscles tensed as he pulled the trigger. I heard a deafening …

… click.

'Shit,' the Iron Mask mumbled, flicking my hand aside. He opened the chamber; it was loaded with nothing but air. 'The bitch stole my bullets again.'

'Don't blame your wife,' the Gorilla said, not taking his eye off the book. 'I willed the bullets away with my mind. It's amazing what nonlinear thinking can accomplish. See?' He held out his massive palm, in the middle of which lay six .22 caliber bullets.

'You son of a bitch, give those back to me!'

'I'm afraid not.' He tossed the bullets out the window.

The Iron Mask clenched his fists and sprang forward. He tried to push me out of the way, apparently not expecting me to punch him in the gut. As he doubled over, I slammed my knee into his testicles. He fell to the floor and curled up into the fetal position. I was more than a little surprised. The 'special' ingredients within the Iron Mask's concoction packed an impressive wallop.

[Memo to driver: we would like our hero to address the audience with a soliloquy of approximately 400 words at some point during the trip. Thank you.]

The atmosphere in the bus grew tense. I could feel a multitude of eyes glaring at me. I found myself studying the other passengers in detail. For the first time I realized how many of them were in constant, irreversible pain. The old woman, the rapper, the married couple, the eagle-man, even the gibbering things in the back. Not one of them was free of pain. They had been born into it, their crippled flesh would hobble through life infested with it, they would die choking on it, the ash-like fragments (the physical manifestation of pain itself) foaming up out of their mouths like the remnants of a volcanic eruption … followed by a long stretch of nothing until the next incarnation when the pain would begin again. Even worse than before.

'Don't worry,' the Gorilla said cheerfully while turning a page in his book. 'It *can* be transcended. All it takes is tapping into one's full potential. That's why I came on this little trip: to find my true Self before it's too late, before I have to make that final excursion into the Great Beyond we all must face in the end.' He held up the little red book. I scanned the title: *101 Things To Do Before You Kick Off.*

'How strange,' I heard myself saying. 'Where did you get that book?'

'I pilfered it from the Royal Institute of International Affairs. That's why I had to leave England so quickly. Oh, believe me, they have quite a lot of interesting tomes tucked safely away inside the Institute walls, quite a lot indeed.'

Since the Iron Mask was still writhing on the floor, I decided to take his seat. 'May I see it?' I said, holding out my palm.

The Gorilla seemed reluctant at first, then relented. 'Oh, all right. But do give it back, please. I'll no doubt be in need of its contents soon.'

I flipped the book open to a random page. The first passage I stumbled across read as follows: 'In order to divorce oneself from the pain of a particularly traumatic memory, one must relive the experience in its entirety.'

I glanced up from the page and stared off into space, giving the words time to settle into my mind. 'I wonder if that's true,' I mumbled softly, to no one in particular.

'Oh, of course it's true,' the Gorilla said.

I jumped at the sound of his voice; I hadn't been expecting a response. 'How do you even know what

I'm talking about?' I glanced down at the book, then pressed the open pages to my chest. 'You don't know what sentence I just read, do you?'

'Oh dear me, no, not at all. However, if I *did* I'd simply tell you this: It's very important to distinguish between an event and the *memory* of that event. It's been scientifically ascertained that the physical effects of emotional trauma last for a maximum of twelve minutes. That's all. Any pain we experience after that has little more substance than a shadow, as with an amputee who insists he can still feel his limbs. In order to transcend the lingering effects of a painful memory, we must learn to disassociate the primary stimulus (nearly drowning in a swimming pool as a child, for example) from the present stimulus (taking a bath, perhaps). To overcome such phobias, one must live through the primary experience again, confront it in such excruciating detail that it loses its power over one's subconscious. Uh, but that's just a guess on my part.' The Gorilla pulled out a copy of *The Sun* newspaper from beneath his seat and began doing the crossword puzzle.

'But wait a second,' I said. 'I'm not like these other people.' I gestured toward the other passengers. 'I don't have any traumatic experiences. I'm not in any *serious* pain, not really.'

'Is that so?' The Gorilla sounded skeptical.

'Of course it's "so"!'

From the Iron Mask on the floor, between clenched teeth, emerged a groan followed by three words: 'What about Elizabeth?'

'Elizabeth?' I said. 'Wh-what do you …?'

185

… lying motionless on a white carpet, her face drenched in blood, her open eyes black as night and staring right through me into another world …

… perhaps this one ….

Yes, of course. Elizabeth.

[Memo to driver: re: theatre of alienation. How would Bertolt Brecht stage the following scene?]

I lowered myself to the floor, sat beside the Iron Mask. I crossed my legs under me and allowed the pent-up words to pour into the air. 'The migraines began … when I was twelve, when my mother died. My father remarried only a month later. What disturbed me the most was how much *nicer* my new mother was. She showered me with kindness, whereas my real mother was something of a tyrant … so much so that I spent my adolescent years wishing her dead. I guess I got my wish, huh?

'My stepmom was so fucking nice I couldn't stand it anymore. On my thirteenth birthday I ran away from home, got mixed up in marijuana, alcohol, heroin (never speed, never needed it), prostitution, rock 'n' roll, blah blah blah. Didn't stop me from getting an education, though. I'd read all the great philosophers before I was seventeen. Nietzsche was my favorite. And the Marquis de Sade, of course. I think I shared a lot in common with the fat old fellow. Pain was the measuring stick I used to judge any experience, no matter what it was: sex, crime, music, food. And love? You can bet that any girl who genuinely loved me got the ol' heave-ho within a couple of months. I can't name how many commitments I've broken. And all for what? To run off with some whore who'd usually end up sticking a shiv in my back the first time I let my guard down? I think I've spent my life running away from … well, from love, I guess. Is that why I hated Elizabeth so much? Is that why I did what I did when she insisted I marry her? Is that why I pushed her just a little too hard, just enough to slam her head into that coffee table, just enough to … to …' I could see it all over again. *The blood*. 'To get her *away* from me, to …' *The blood*. There was so little of it and yet—she wasn't moving. She wasn't moving at all. Yes, yes that was the moment. That was when I first saw the curtain, hovering like a ghost over her prostrate body. The apparition scared me so much I … 'I didn't think. I just got the hell out of there. I swung the duffel bag over my shoulder and *ran* … onto this bus. Jesus, I don't think I've ever run so quickly before. Except … except when I … ran away from … home.'

For the first time in my life, I felt tears moistening my cheeks. Before I knew it, I was on my hands and knees sobbing into the gum-and-Pepsi-stained floor. I'm not sure how long that lasted. Too long, probably. I've been told I never know when to quit being maudlin.

[Memo to driver: please allow for a brief silence here. This is not a suggestion.]

Abruptly, the sound of applause. Every passenger on the bus was clapping, including the Man in the Iron Mask. He was laughing too. In between his guffaws he said: 'Aw, don't let this nonsense worry you, kid. Women are scum. If I cried over every bitch I put in the hospital I'd have enough tears to fill the L.A. River. Look at my old lady. Before I left on this little trip I had to drop her off at the Emergency Room—where she belongs. You can't trust anybody, kid. Not your girlfriend, not the government, not the Good Humor Man. Just get used to it.'

The Gorilla yawned. 'My, aren't we pessimistic today.'

'Why the hell shouldn't I be? This son of a bitch just kicked me in the nuts! What did I do to deserve that?'

The Gorilla rolled his eyes, then shifted his considerable weight toward me. Holding his index finger in the air, he said, 'Keep in mind, young sir, there's always a new day dawning.'

The Iron Mask rose to his feet and leaned into the Gorilla's furry face. 'What is this, a musical? You know what's going on inside this bus as well I do! Spare us the Pollyanna crap, okay? Why don't you go talk to the fucking driver if everything's so god damn optimistic!'

The Gorilla didn't respond this time; he just retreated behind his crossword puzzle. Seeing him do this made me uneasy. My respect for him dwindled.

Once again I found myself glancing at that curtain, that *strange curtain* ....

The Iron Mask, following my gaze, laughed hysterically. 'You know where we're going don't you, kid? Sure you do. Hee. We're all going to the same place. In the end. In the end. If you're lucky you'll get to see your Elizabeth again soon.'

The Gorilla snatched his book out of my hand. He

closed his eyes and clutched it to his massive chest like a mother with her newborn child. He was chanting something, I don't know what. It sounded like a prayer.

I glanced back at the passengers. Focused on the kid with the NO FEAR t-shirt. Yes, that sounded like a good idea. No fear.

I stood up. I approached the curtain …

'No!' the Gorilla screamed. 'Just leave it alone!'

The Iron Mask tried to drown him out: 'Go for it, kid! Let's get to the truth. Let's see the little man behind the fucking curtain! Do it, kid, *do it*!'

I didn't need any encouragement from the Iron Mask. I pulled the curtain aside with a violent jerk, and at that instant

[Memo to driver: turn the lights directly upon the audience. Blind them.]

the searing light of the world beyond the windshield subsumed my vision. There was nothing outside. No reptiles, no tumbleweeds, no cacti, no highway, no desert, no mountains, no sky. No earth. No Elizabeth. In that final second before I lost my vision, I saw the driver's face in the polished rearview mirror.

He had no eyes.

This Time

Antonia Rachel Ward

'Ten …! Nine …! Eight …!'

The roar of the crowd echoes in my ears. I stumble through the crush of sweaty bodies, tripping over feet, dodging raised glasses of champagne. Somebody grabs my arm and I whirl round to find Vicki thrusting a drink at me.

'Seven …! Six …! Five …!'

'Come on!' she shrieks. Her face is pink and beaming, her eyes smudged with mascara. 'It's almost time!'

'I've got to find Alex,' I shout, scanning the crowd for his messy hair. Panic tightens my chest.

'Fuck Alex.' Vicki's fingers claw at my blouse. 'It's the millennium, Thea. You can't miss it!'

'Four …! Three ….! Two …!'

Shoving Vicki aside, I stumble through the back door into the night, just as the pub explodes into a lairy rendition of 'Auld Lang Syne'. The door swings closed, muffling the sound, and suddenly I'm alone in the deserted beer garden.

'Alex!' I run down the grass slope that leads to the riverside, between picnic tables covered in half-empty glasses. 'Alex, where are you?!'

When I reach the Thames, I scan the garden, heart hammering. Empty benches. Abandoned bottles. Smoldering cigarette stubs. Above me, the pub windows glow in the darkness. He's nowhere. He's gone.

The river's running fast, moonlight glittering on its surface like a sprinkling of stars. If he jumped in there he'd have been swept away by the current. For a moment, I don't want to believe it, yet his words earlier were warning enough: 'Thea … I can't find the light.'

My breath mists in the freezing air. I thought I'd got it right this time. It's been six months—longer than ever before. But I feel the now-familiar tug in the centre of my stomach, and it tells me without a doubt: Alex is dead. Again.

The pub garden dissolves around me. The sound of 'Auld Lang Syne' grows fainter, then vanishes. I know where I'm going—back to the beginning—and I know where it will all end, because it's always the same. Every time.

~

He stands under the sodium glow of the streetlamp, one foot against the silver pole, shoulders slightly hunched. A cigarette dangles from his lips, unlit. He flicks his lighter one, two, three times, and a flame flares, only to sputter out in the fine spray of drizzle. He shakes it, swears under his breath, tries again.

I watch him from the bus stop, holding my umbrella at a slant. I wonder which of us will be the first to approach. Him, or me? The thought crosses my mind that perhaps this time, neither of us will. Perhaps the bus will arrive, and I will get on it, and he will continue his solitary walk home, smoking his cigarette. Perhaps this will be the occasion our paths do not cross.

Even as I think it, the thought seems impossible. Our paths always cross. It is inevitable. The natural order of things.

As he finally manages to light his cigarette, he looks up, and for one blinding instant our eyes meet. The night illuminates; the dark and light swap places like the negative of a photograph. I glance away, and the world turns black again. Rain drums on the perspex wall of the bus stop. Beneath its flimsy roof, two older ladies have taken the only seats, so I stand outside of its shelter, one foot crossed in front of the other, crumpled ticket clutched in my free hand.

My ticket to freedom.

What a cliché. My ticket to a different sort of prison, perhaps. When I walked out on my fiancé, I left with nothing but a holdall. Scattered behind me are disappointed dreams, like a collection of faded Polaroids. Ahead, only grey clouds of uncertainty. Whatever happened to the belief I used to have that I could be anything? Do anything?

A car zips down the silent street, sending up a splash

of water. From the corner of my eye, I notice him turn, take a step in the direction of home. I want to cry out to him. *Don't go. Don't leave. Choose me.*

Is it his turn, or mine? At some point I lost track. But here's the bus, coming along the road with its windows glowing, and he's got his back to me, walking away. In a few moments he'll round the corner. I'll get on the bus. It'll be over before it's even begun.

Then I notice something small and silver shining beneath the streetlamp. His lighter. He must have dropped it. I seize my chance, dart over to pick it up, and run after him.

'I think this is yours.' I thrust the lighter into his hand.

'Thank you.' He glances at it, then me, then the bus. The ladies are already climbing aboard. 'You're going to miss your bus.'

'It doesn't matter,' I say, trying to keep the relief out of my voice. 'I was going nowhere, anyway.'

The rain is picking up, and here, out of the warmth of the streetlamp, the red embers of his cigarette are the only light. I can't see his face for shadows, but I know it all the same. Heavy brows, knitted into a permanent frown, framing chocolate brown eyes. Sharp cheek-bones. Smooth, honey-golden skin. His hair is a shock of unruly black that never lays flat no matter how much he brushes it. It's a face I've seen a thousand times—and none.

As my bus sails by, he nods towards the nearest pub, a faux-Irish tavern with a green and gold sign, hung with baskets of flowers. 'I'll buy you a drink while you wait for the next one.'

The pub smells of beer and stale tobacco, but it has a homely glow. A few tables are occupied by couples tucking into fish and chips, while a tired barmaid trades banter and forced smiles with a small knot of locals. Somebody's decorated the specials board with chalk-drawn shamrocks. My new friend shrugs off his heavy woollen coat and takes a seat opposite a green leather couch. I put my holdall on the floor and slide along the couch until I'm facing him.

'What can I get you?' he asks.

'Oh, it's OK. I can …'

He waves my protest away. He's younger than me, with a studenty look about him: slightly unkempt, like he's not yet learned to look after himself properly. His uncertain smile makes me want to surround him in bubble wrap and protect him from the world.

'Let me guess.' He peers at me as if trying to read my mind. 'White wine … No. Tonic with a dash of lime.'

He's right, of course. Second time. And it makes me wonder whether somewhere, in some deep core of his being, he remembers. I catch his eye, and he holds my gaze for a long moment. A faint look of puzzlement crosses his face.

'I'm Alex, by the way.'

I smile. I know.

How did we get here? Is this the hundredth time I've missed my bus? The thousandth? I stopped keeping track long ago. All the memories fade into one another. The time I tripped on my way up the bus steps, and Alex rushed over to help me up. The time he dropped his phone in the gutter and I was so busy trying to help him, I didn't even notice the bus until it drove away. Once, he was inexplicably late, and we very nearly missed each other completely. But we always found each other. Every time.

While Alex is at the bar, I toy with the lighter he left on the table, running my thumb over the engraved pattern on the silver. He doesn't know it, but it was a gift from me. I scoured antique shops for days until I found the perfect one. I turn it over to read the inscription on the back.

> *Now you always have a light,*
> *Thea.*

Alex returns to the table, drinks in hand.

'What did you say your name was?' He slides my glass over to me.

'I didn't. It's Thea.'

'Coincidence.' He smiles, nodding towards the lighter.

Not really. I got that engraving done myself, at the key cutter's not ten minutes' walk from here. In a different world. A different life. On a few occasions, I've tried to explain this to him, but it's difficult for him to understand. As far as he's concerned, he's always had it. He never thinks to question where it came from. I suppose it's difficult for me to understand, too. All I really know is that I'm here, repeating my life over and over again in different ways, waiting for one thing.

Waiting for the reality where I don't lose him.

'Wish I knew what the engraving meant,' he muses, tucking the lighter back into his pocket.

'Something to do with finding hope in a dark place?' I hazard.

Alex's lip twitches. 'It's a nice sentiment.'

He glances at the darkened window, looking out onto the night with that faraway stare I've come to know so well. It's hard to resist the urge to skip the small talk when I know what troubles him, and all I want to do is make it better. But I've learnt from experience that if I wade straight in I only scare him. 'How can you see so much in me,' he asked me once, 'when I can't even see it myself?' No, to get Alex to open up takes patience. Like unlocking an intricate puzzle. But if something's worth doing, it's worth taking time over.

I might as well. It would seem I have all the time in the world.

Amongst the haze of memories, the first time stands out to me as clearly as polished silver. I've run over it in my mind so many times, it's become worn to a shine. That was the one time I wasn't looking for him. My focus was fixed on the argument I'd just had with my fiancé, the sound of our raised voices ringing inside my skull. I had no time for the scruffy student-type who sloped up beside me.

'D'you have a light?'

I shook my head. 'Don't smoke, sorry.'

'Probably wise.' He grinned at the floor and ran a hand through his hair. 'Filthy habit.'

The bus pulled up, and the two older ladies got up from their seats. They squeezed between me and Alex as the doors hissed open. The passing of each body between us felt so unwelcome that I was glad when they were gone. Alex must have sensed my hesitation. I hoisted my holdall onto my shoulder with a faint smile, and was about to get on the bus myself when he said, 'There'll be another one in an hour, you know.'

And that was that. The beginning of six months of discovering one another, peeling away the layers we'd built up as protection from the outside world, hunting hungrily for the little flashes of the true selves within. Neither of us were very forthcoming. I was hurt; he was guarded. We had disagreements, misunderstandings, moments of intense, giddy relief when we made up. I all but moved in to his little third-floor flat, with its scent of vinyl and freshly brewed coffee. Not that there was much space for me between his record collection and his mixing deck. All he had to sleep on was a mattress on the floor.

Alex wanted to be a DJ. Not just the spinning-tracks-in-a-club sort of DJ, but an artist. A creator, weaving beats and melodies together like poetry, to create something entirely new and unexpected. He approached it with the dedication of an obsessive, spending long nights hunched over his computer, headphones on, so focused that it would've taken an earthquake to disturb him. I barely made a ripple in his consciousness during those times, floating behind him like a ghost, bringing him mugs of coffee and egg sandwiches. But to me, he was a river I could drown in. I forgot my destination. I forgot my life, my friends, my own dream of opening an art gallery. And when I woke one morning to find nothing left of him but a note on the kitchen table, I

197

realised he'd taken a chunk of my soul along with him.

The note read simply:

I couldn't find the light.

~

'Ever feel like you're fighting to keep putting one foot in front of the other, to get to a destination you're not sure you even want to reach?' Alex asks. We've been sitting in the Irish pub for hours, and it's almost closing time. The air has a heaviness to it—stillness waiting to fall. The barmaid wipes down tables. Only a couple of the locals remain, propping up the bar.

'Yes.' There was a time I wouldn't have understood what Alex meant. We were so happy. So in love. I had an optimism about life that I'd never had in any of my previous relationships. For the first time, I knew how it felt to be with someone who was truly on my side. Because no matter what happened, whatever he said or didn't say, he was always there for me. He never let me down. And in return, I poured my whole soul into loving him. Supported him. Encouraged him. Picked him up every time he was rejected by record producers. I was the one who told him to keep fighting. Keep putting one foot in front of the other. No matter how far away from his dream he seemed to get, he always had me. So how could he be so despondent?

Now I understand. I've walked this road many times before, and every time it gets harder. Every time there's a destination ahead of me that I'm not sure I want to reach—the one where Alex dies. Every time the hope that keeps me going gets dimmer. I'm not sure even I can find the light anymore.

Alex puts another cigarette in his mouth, flicks his lighter so that the flame flares. As he lights the cigarette, he asks, 'Where were you going, anyway? On that bus?'

'Nowhere,' I reply.

'That's what you said earlier.'

That's all I ever say.

I've never told him where I was going, or even where I came from. Not in any version of reality. It never seems important. All that matters to me is the two of us. After a while, he gives up asking. But this time, he turns to me, locking his gaze on mine, and the thought flashes through my mind: He knows.

'You're going nowhere right now, Thea,' he says. 'You know it. There'll be one more bus along in'—he checks his watch—'...fifteen minutes. Last bus of the night. How about you catch it?'

'I … I can't.'

'Why not?' Alex takes a drag of his cigarette, and his smile flickers.

How? How can I say: Because you're going to die, by your own hand, at some point in the next six months, and I need to stop you. How can I possibly explain that? But I don't have to because, before long, he speaks again.

'You've got a life to live out there, don't you? Perhaps it's about time you went out and lived it. I've got some shit to work out, by myself. I'll find you when I'm ready.'

While I hesitate, he adds, 'Better be quick. You don't have much time.'

And it occurs to me that this is the one thing I've never tried. In this repeating loop, I've done everything I can possibly think of to help Alex. I've given him everything I know how to give. But the one thing I haven't tried is letting him go. It's all I've got left.

I scribble my number on the back of a placemat.

'Look me up,' I say. 'When you're ready.'

He smiles. Tucks the placemat into his pocket. 'I'll do that.'

Ten minutes later, I'm on the bus to nowhere.

A year passes, then two, and I don't hear from Alex. I resist the urge to look him up. If he died, surely my loop would restart. I would know. And so I imagine him, building his own life, just as I'm building mine, and I try to trust him to be there when he's ready.

~

'Five …! Four …! Three …! Two …! One!'

HAPPY NEW YEAR 2010.

The banner hangs above my head, covering half the gallery wall. This is a dual celebration—the new year, and my gallery's grand opening. A group of friends descend upon me, drawing me into a giddy hug, starting up a drunken rendition of 'Auld Lang Syne'. I am buffeted this way and that, hands grabbing at mine to link me into a chain. To my left, warm fingers wrap around mine, and I know.

I just know.

The smell of vinyl and fresh coffee, and cigarette smoke. I turn to look at him, and he smiles.

'Have we met?'

About the Authors

William F. Aicher is the author of *The Trouble With Being God*, *A Confession*, *The Unfortunate Expiration of Mr. David S. Sparks*, *Calibration 74*, and the Phoenix Bones: International Monster Hunter series, as well as a series of short horror and suspense pieces collectively referred to as 'Creepy Little Bedtime Stories.' Tending to lean toward the creepy and fantastical, his work has appeared alongside such well-known writers as Stephen King, Richard Chizmar, and Neil Gaiman. A graduate of the University of Wisconsin, Madison, he holds degrees in journalism and philosophy. He currently lives outside Milwaukee with his wife, three sons, and a pair of lazy cats.

Writer, poet and podcaster **Jasmine Arch** lives and writes in a green little nook of Belgium, with two elderly horses, entirely too many dogs, and a husband who knows better than to distract her when she's spinning tales. Her work has appeared in *Hybrid Fiction*, *NewMyths.com*, and *The Other Stories*. Find out more about her or her work at jasminearch.com.

Mark Bolsover's work represents a form of Modernist-inspired experimentation in psychological realism and prose-poetry, aiming to break apart conventional uses of language which serve to mask experience. He is a winner of the Into the Void Poetry Award (2016). His debut chapbook, *IN FAILURE & IN RUINS—dreams & fragments*, is published with Into the Void Press (2017). His first collection, *contra FLUX.—moments caught (arrested) whilst in-from motion.*, is published with Polyversity Press (2019). His work has appeared in a number of international literary publications, including *Into the Void*, *Projectionist's Playground*, *SPAM Zine*, *Mycelia*, *Open Polyversity*, and *Poetry Bus*.

A member of the Horror Writers Association, **R. A. Busby**'s story 'Street View' (Collective Realms #2) was recently selected for inclusion on the Preliminary Ballot List for the Bram Stoker Awards for 2020. She has several other published horror stories including 'Bits' (Short Sharp Shocks #43), the Shirley Jackson Award-nominated 'Holes' (Women in Horror Anthology #2: Graveyard

Smash), 'Kiss' (Women in Horror Anthology #3: The One That Got Away), 'A Short, Happy Life' (Creepy Podcast 12/20), and 'Ill Wind' (Anomalies and Curiosities). A horror fan since early childhood, R. A. Busby spends her spare time running in the desert with her dog and finding weird things to write about.

Merl Fluin lives on the Isle of Wight, UK, where she thinks about weird fiction and tends her blog, *Gorgon In Furs* (gorgoninfurs.com). She is the author of the Surrealist Western novel *The Golden Cut*, and her poetry and prose have been published in numerous Surrealist books and magazines. Her most recent short story appeared in *Dark Lane Anthology Volume 10*.

Robert Guffey's books include *Widow of the Amputation and Other Weird Crimes* (Eraserhead Press, 2021), *Bela Lugosi's Dead* (Crossroad Press, 2021), *Until the Last Dog Dies* (Night Shade/Skyhorse, 2017), *Chameleo: A Strange but True Story of Invisible Spies, Heroin Addiction, and Homeland Security* (OR Books, 2015), *Spies & Saucers* (PS Publishing, 2014), and *Cryptoscatology: Conspiracy Theory as Art Form* (TrineDay, 2012). He's written stories and articles for numerous magazines and anthologies, among them *The Believer, Black Dandy, The Evergreen Review, The Los Angeles Review of Books, The Mailer Review, Phantom Drift, Postscripts, Rosebud, Salon,* and *TOR.com*.

Ayd Instone is head of Physics at Fyling Hall School in Robin Hood's Bay. He has written various books on creative thinking and a textbook *Exam Insights for GCSE Physics* for Hodder Education. His Lovecraftian story 'The Wall' was published in *Mythos: 16* by tiger-sharkpublishing.com. He has published two volumes of short science fiction and ghost stories *The Voice in the Light* and *On the Shores of Lake Onyx*. Find him on Twitter @aydinstone.

Thomas Kendall's previous work has appeared in *Userlands* (Akashic press) edited by Dennis Cooper and online at *Entropy* and *lies/isle*. His debut novel *The Autodidacts* is published by Whiskey Tit press. His Twitter is @tpkendall.

Tomas Marcantonio is the author of the dystopian noir trilogy *Sonaya Nights* from Storgy Books. His short stories and poetry have appeared in numerous anthologies and literary magazines, and in 2020 he was nominated for the Pushcart Prize and Best of the Net awards. Tomas splits his time between the seaside cities of Busan, South Korea, and Brighton, England.

David McAllister is a writer of thought-provoking fiction. His first short story collection *Parallel Worlds and Possible Futures* was released in 2019. He has several published stories and articles in *Doctor Who* and other

TV series-based books and websites. He lives in Wallasey with his wife and four sons.

Ross McCleary is from Edinburgh. His work has appeared in *Structo, Litro,* and *Extra Teeth*. In 2019 he was awarded a New Writer's Award for Fiction from the Scottish Book Trust. In the same year his debut poetry pamphlet, *Endorse Me, You Cowards!,* was published by Stewed Rhubarb Press.

L. P. Melling currently writes from Bedfordshire after academia and a legal career took him around the country. His fiction appears in such places as *Dark Matter Magazine*, *Frozen Wavelets*, the *Upon a Twice Time* anthology, and *Best of British Science Fiction 2020*. When not writing, he works for a legal charity in Cambridge. You can find out more about him at his site, which includes a sporadically maintained blog: lpmelling.wordpress. com.

Soumya Sundar Mukherjee is an admirer of engaging sci-fi, horror and fantasy tales. A bi-lingual writer from West Bengal, India, he writes about stuff strange dreams are made of. His works of fiction have appeared in *Mother of Invention Anthology*, *Reckoning Magazine* and a few other places. He lives in Midnapore Town of Bengal province of India with his twelve family members: four humans and eight cats.

Kurt Newton's fiction has appeared in numerous magazines and anthologies, including *Weird Tales*, *Weirdbook*, *Vastarien*, *Nightscript*, *Cafe Irreal*, *Penumbric* and *Cosmic Horror Monthly*.

Stephen Oram writes science fiction. He is a founding curator for near-future fiction at Virtual Futures and a member of the Clockhouse London Writers. He works with artists, scientists and technologists to explore possible future outcomes of their research through short stories and is a writer for sci-fi prototypers SciFutures. He is published in several anthologies and has two published novels. His collections *Eating Robots* and *Biohacked & Begging* have been praised by publications as diverse as *The Morning Star* and *The Financial Times*.

Nadia Steven Rysing (she/her) is a poet and speculative writer living on the Haldimand Tract in Southwestern Ontario. Her work has appeared in *Black Telephone Magazine*, *FUTURES*, and under a previous name in *No Place For Us*, *Spirit's Tincture*, *Wizards in Space*, *Eye to the Telescope*, and *Strange Constellations*. You can find her on Twitter @a_tendency.

Having trained as an astronomer and subsequently managed an industrial research group, **Vaughan Stanger** now writes sci-fi and fantasy fiction full-time. He enjoys swimming but steadfastly maintains that he has never met Janine. His short stories have appeared in *Interzone*, *Daily Science Fiction*, *Abyss & Apex*, *Postscripts*, and *Nature Futures*, among others, and have been collected in *Moondust Memories*, *Sons of the Earth & Other Stories*, and *The Last Moonshot & Other Stories*. Follow his writing adventures at vaughanstanger.com or on Twitter @vaughanstanger.

Antonia Rachel Ward is an author of historical gothic romance and horror, based in Cambridgeshire, UK. Her short stories and flash fiction have been published by Black Hare Press and Gypsum Sound Tales, among others. Her poetry is forthcoming in Blackspot Books' *Under the Skin,* an anthology of body horror poetry by women. She is also the founder and editor-in-chief of Ghost Orchid Press. She has recently completed an erotic horror novella, Marionette, and is currently working on a gothic romance novel. You can find her on Twitter @antoniarachelw1, Instagram @antoniarachelward, or at antoniarachelward.com.

About the Editor

C.R. Dudley is a visual artist, writer, and mind explorer. She is fascinated by the human condition, in particular the effect future technological developments might have on the psyche, and sees everything she creates as part of one continuous artwork.

She started blogging in 2014 as a way to express the ideas stemming from her studies in Jungian psychology, philosophy and various schools of mysticism. Her first few stories were distributed as hand-stitched art zines in aid of a mental health charity, and her style became known for its multi-layered narratives.

In 2017 she founded Orchid's Lantern, a small independent press focusing on the metaphysical and visionary genre. She is the author of two short story collections, *Fragments of Perception* (2017) and *Mind in the Gap* (2018), as well as a forthcoming series of novels inspired by the workings of the unconscious mind.

C.R. Dudley lives in North Yorkshire with her husband and daughter, and is a lover of forest walks, pizza, tequila and dark music.

Vast: Stories of Mind, Soul and Consciousness in a Technological Age

Edited by C.R. Dudley

Ten exciting, thought-provoking science fiction stories exploring the relationship between cutting-edge technology and the human psyche. What would it mean for an artificial brain to become conscious? Is awareness always tethered to the body? Could we ever accept a virtual reality as our own? Perhaps our minds already have more impact on the fabric of reality than we realise...

With contributions from:

Stephen Oram	Jonathan D. Clark
J.R. Staples-Ager	Ellinor Kall
Thomas Cline	Ava Kelly
Vaughan Stanger	Peter Burton
Sergio Palumbo	Juliane Graef

Printed in Great Britain
by Amazon

10293828R10123